LIZZY JAMES

Do I Look Amused?

A Sweet Romantic Comedy

Copyright © 2022 by Lizzy James

All rights reserved. No part of this publication may be reproduced, stored or transmitted in any form or by any means, electronic, mechanical, photocopying, recording, scanning, or otherwise without written permission from the publisher. It is illegal to copy this book, post it to a website, or distribute it by any other means without permission.

This novel is entirely a work of fiction. The names, characters and incidents portrayed in it are the work of the author's imagination. Any resemblance to actual persons, living or dead, events or localities is entirely coincidental.

Designations used by companies to distinguish their products are often claimed as trademarks. All brand names and product names used in this book and on its cover are trade names, service marks, trademarks and registered trademarks of their respective owners. The publishers and the book are not associated with any product or vendor mentioned in this book. None of the companies referenced within the book have endorsed the book.

First edition

ISBN: 9798814522245

This book was professionally typeset on Reedsy. Find out more at reedsy.com

*In memory of Little Girl,
our toy poodle and itty-bitty clown
who passed during the writing of this book.
I will forever miss your unconditional love and devotion,
your sweet brown eyes, and your soft cuddles.*

Contents

Foreword — iii
Acknowledgement — iv
Chapter One: Claire — 1
Chapter Two: Claire — 7
Chapter Three: Ryan — 12
Chapter Four: Ryan — 19
Chapter Five: Claire — 25
Chapter Six: Ryan — 32
Chapter Seven: Ryan — 37
Chapter Eight: Claire — 42
Chapter Nine: Ryan — 49
Chapter Ten: Ryan — 56
Chapter Eleven: Claire — 62
Chapter Twelve: Claire — 68
Chapter Thirteen: Ryan — 73
Chapter Fourteen: Ryan — 79
Chapter Fifteen: Claire — 84
Chapter Sixteen: Claire — 89
Chapter Seventeen: Ryan — 94
Chapter Eighteen: Ryan — 99
Chapter Nineteen: Claire — 105
Chapter Twenty: Claire — 112
Chapter Twenty-One: Claire — 117
Chapter Twenty-Two: Ryan — 122

Chapter Twenty-Three: Ryan	127
Chapter Twenty-Four: Claire	133
Chapter Twenty-Five: Claire	137
Chapter Twenty-Six: Ryan	143
Chapter Twenty-Seven: Ryan	148
Chapter Twenty-Eight: Claire	153
Chapter Twenty-Nine: Claire	158
Chapter Thirty: Claire	164
Chapter Thirty-One: Ryan	169
Chapter Thirty-Two: Claire	177
Chapter Thirty-Three: Claire	183
Chapter Thirty-Four: Ryan	189
Chapter Thirty-Five: Claire	195
Chapter Thirty-Six: Ryan	202
Epilogue: Claire	210
About the Author	212
Also by Lizzy James	214

Foreword

Dear Reader,

    I hope you enjoy reading *Do I Look Amused?* as much as I enjoyed writing it! Please consider leaving a review on Amazon, Goodreads, and any other book-related sites when you're finished. It would mean the world to me.

    Trigger warning: This novel deals with the death of a parent, but from the beginning, it was my goal to keep that portion of the story light. While Ryan and his family do grieve the loss of his father, I chose to focus on the happy memories and the idea that he wanted his family to move on after he passed. Much discussion was exchanged between myself and my alpha readers to make sure a comfortable balance was achieved. I truly hope that if you've lost a parent or spouse, you'll find comfort in Ryan, Travis, and their mother Helene's journey.

Happy Reading!
Lizzy James
aka Elizabeth J. Smith

Acknowledgement

Thank you to Leah and Jonathan
for letting me bounce ideas off of you at all hours
and for answering those *awkward* questions.
IYKYK

Thank you to my patrons,
Gail S. and Kate J.
for helping me live my author dreams!

Chapter One: Claire

Early June, Pony Island, South Carolina

"Reynaldo! Get out of the women's restroom!"
The flurry of feathers and talons – *wait, do peacocks have talons?*

"Ouch!" Claire Hensley gasped as what could only be a talon sliced the shoulder of her favorite crepe blouse, grazing her skin. "You little snot!"

Squawk! Reynaldo's beady black eyes showed no remorse as he spread his tail feathers, hitting Claire in the face with *eau de peacock*. The acrid whiff of bird poop and, well, *bird* almost made her lose her lunch.

"Are you all right in there, Claire?" called Kendra Lanier, her best friend and the Pony Island Amusement Park's amazing secretary. The girl had the energy of a Boykin Spaniel, along with the state dog's sweet demeanor, something Claire couldn't claim at the moment. "Should I call security?"

"No!" Claire replied, feeling a mental jab. They'd already cut crew wages by ten percent. Chasing vain peacocks was off the officers' list of charitable contributions to a dying employer. "We'll figure this out."

The Sea-Horse popped its head in, the huge fuzzy white body, clad in a metallic shell bikini and mermaid tail, blocking all the natural light. Reynaldo shook his plumage like a rattler.

"Miss Claire, do you think he'd follow my shiny tail?"

"We can try it, Jacob." The teen boy's voice coming out of the park's mascot always made her smile. "Give us a good swish!"

Spinning around, Jacob jerked the mermaid tail back and forth, reminding Claire more of a fish out of water than a graceful kelpie. Reynaldo was not impressed, backing farther into the restroom.

"There's another restroom by the Ferris wheel," Claire heard Kendra say. "No, this doesn't happen all that often."

The South Carolina sun caught a scale on the Sea-Horse's tail, blinding Claire. Reynaldo chose that moment to back into her, the brownish feathers on the reverse side of his – admittedly impressive – tail brushing her nose.

"Yuck! I love you, buddy, but you stink! I don't see how your harem stands you."

Squawk, squawk! (You don't smell all that great yourself, human!)

Claire squeezed out from behind the bird. "Stop, Jacob! It's not working. We need a new plan."

"Maybe if we herd over one of the peahens?" Kendra called, her espresso curls backdropped by the gorgeous afternoon. What Claire wouldn't give to be out there, smelling the salty sea air – rather than Sir Stinky. "Or I could grab some of his feed."

Claire checked her watch. Reynaldo's head jerked toward her. *Was he fixin' to attack?* She splayed her hands in an attempt to placate. Boredom replaced his curious tilt. On a hunch, she displayed her vintage-style timepiece. The peacock perked up.

"You like my watch, do you?" she asked, unhooking it from her wrist. Tick-tocking her body in time with the swinging watch, she backed

Chapter One: Claire

toward the entrance. "Come on, little buddy. Come on out of there."

Squawk? (If I obey, will you give it to me?)

"Not on your life," she muttered. Reynaldo shook his tail in defiance before the swinging pendulum's spell again subjected him. "Follow the sound of my voice. You want to be outside where everyone can admire you, don't you?"

The peacock stepped forward. Claire took a step back, then another.

"You're such a handsome boy, aren't you?" she crooned, stroking his ego. He nodded, taking two steps this time. "The handsomest peacock on the island...no, all of South Carolina!"

Reynaldo froze, challenge in his hard glare.

"In all the world," she added, rolling her eyes. This met his approval. A few seconds later, he was out. The small audience of crew and guests cheered. A woman with a squirming toddler scurried through, not bothering to watch her steps. *Ew.* Kendra threw her arm around Claire's shoulders.

"I'm going to call you the peacock whisperer from now on." Then, she gagged. "Oh, gross! You smell like Reynaldo."

"I know," Claire replied, catching her friend by the waist so she couldn't escape the stench. "Wanna help me clean up? There's poop ev-er-y-where."

Kendra peeled herself away. "No, I'm good."

"Suit yourself."

"Miss Claire, is my shift over?" Jacob asked, the Sea-Horse's head sagging. "This suit is murder in the sun."

"Go ahead, Jacob," she replied, noting the stain on the mermaid tail. *Add that to my list.* "I think we've all had enough for one day."

* * *

Claire loved this time of the day. Right after the last guest passed

3

through the gates and all of the rides shut down for the night, a hush fell over the park, draping it in an ethereal state of half-slumber. A twilight of blues, oranges, and reds danced with the first specks of star over the ocean waves, their crash and flow audible again.

"Don't get me wrong," she whispered to her late grandmother's beloved Carou-Sail, the hand-painted ponies frozen mid-canter. "I love this park more than anything in the world, but it's times like this when I get you all to myself."

Nodding a goodbye to the carousel attendant, she climbed aboard a stormy dapple gray adorned with pearlescent seashells. Stroking the familiar mane, Claire was transported back to her childhood once again. A time of prosperity and excitement. A time without worries. A time without bills to pay and employees to manage.

"Ugh. Can't I just enjoy this?"

Ding, ding! A text sounded from the pocket of her yellow polka-dotted A-line skirt. Her mom.

Natalie: How about dinner tonight? I'm at the market. Lasagna or clams with spaghetti?

Claire: Lasagna. Thanks, Mom. It's been a rough day.

Natalie: I heard. *laughing emoji*

Claire: *tongue stuck out* I was going to shower and change my clothes, but now… *poop*

Natalie: *tears streaming down face* Dinner won't be ready for at least 2 hours. You have time. Love you!

Claire: If you insist. *laughing* Love you too, Mom. *heart*

Dismounting, Claire continued on her way back to the office. The evening maintenance crew was out power-washing the sidewalks and performing routine check-ups on the rides. The Eye of the Hurricane, a popular Gravitron-style ride, had been out of order for three seasons. It was doubtful it would come back online this year.

She exchanged a few words with the crew, thanking them profusely for their commitment to the park. Not everyone stayed after the first pay cuts due to the poor economy, so those who remained were worth their weight in oysters to the Hensley and Lanier families.

We might have to start paying them in oysters, she mused as she reached the office, *unless we can find a pearl.*

* * *

"My, my, child. Your dog run away?" Miss Hattie Reed, the long-time cook at Piper's, the park's sit-down restaurant named after the ubiquitous sandpiper, asked the next afternoon. Like clockwork, she set a cup of hot oolong and a few homemade ginger biscuits on the table in the commercial kitchen. Claire sipped gratefully before grabbing a cookie.

"Numbers are down," she replied. "We're at sixty percent capacity today."

"It is a little overcast," Miss Hattie said, pushing the plate closer. "And I heard there was a yacht race today off the mainland."

"Maybe." Nibble, nibble. "I ate dinner with Mom last night. Helene is worried that Mr. Lanier will have a second heart attack. Even with his time off, his blood pressure is too high. The medicine isn't working either."

"He's in the good Lord's hands, Miss Claire, and I've never known Him to do wrong."

"Nor I, but it's hard to imagine the park without his carefree smile. When Dad died and Mom passed their half of park ownership to me, I wasn't sure I was ready. Mr. Lanier has been so encouraging, along with Jack, and he's fixin' to retire." She lowered her cookie. "I guess the Lanier half will pass to Travis and Kendra."

"Hm." Miss Hattie went to refresh the tea carafes, leaving Claire alone with her thoughts. By the time she returned, ginger-scented crumbs littered the plate. "More cookies?"

"No, ma'am, but thank you." Claire pushed to her feet and threw her arms around the diminutive yet motherly-plump woman. Miss Hattie's hugs were like balm to a weary soul. "I'd best get going. Maybe things have picked up."

"I hope so, child, but always remember: when a door closes, somewhere, the Lord opens a window." Miss Hattie held her at arm's length. "What shampoo are you using?"

"Coconut."

"It ain't strong enough, sugar, to combat Reynaldo."

After they parted, Claire found herself smiling. Leave it to Miss Hattie to soothe wounds and lift spirits. The woman was truly a Godsend.

Chapter Two: Claire

"Claire, the Seagull Scrambler is acting up again," Jack Allison called through the walkie-talkie app on their phones, his deep voice ending with a squeak.

"I'll be right over," she relayed back, hustling from the office in her red tennies. They were a perfect match to her cherry bow blouse and complemented her straight aqua skirt perfectly. She'd even painted her nails to match. Victory Red, it was called. Well, she needed some victory, and fast.

After stopping to give directions to an energetic family of eight and helping a lady and her grandson with the water fountain, Claire arrived at the ride in a pant. The ginormous seagull was suspended mid-swoop, while the crab cars scurried underneath, their seats empty. She apologized to the few guests waiting not-so-patiently in line before finding her boss in the control booth.

"Harvey's broken down again?" she asked, referring to the ancient bird. "Can we fix him before closing?"

"I'm not sure," Jack replied, running a hand over his salt and pepper hair.

Claire let out a groan all the way from the tips of her toes. "If the rest of the ride is working, can we fix him later? Let these people on?"

Her boss casually crossed his arms. "You know company policy. If one part of the ride isn't working, we don't let anyone on. It's not safe. You never know what else might break down."

"I know, but I couldn't help asking." She tapped a fist on her other palm. "This is so frustrating! First, the Eye, and now this. If it keeps up, we'll have the most *unamusing* park in the world!"

"I'm sorry, kid. Let's tell these guests the bad news, and then, we can talk."

She followed Jack out to the queue and pasted on a smile. By the sour faces waiting for them, their news wasn't going to be well received.

"Sorry, folks," Jack said, shaking his head. "The Seagull's out for the night. We'll do our best to have it running by tomorrow morning."

"What good will that do us?" asked a dad of four. "We're heading home tomorrow."

"This place is lame," said his teenaged son, swishing his green and black hair. "I should've stayed at the cabin."

"Yeah," replied his older sister, snapping a depressed-face selfie. *She's probably going to post that on social media*, Claire thought with a cringe. "I'm going to tell all my friends not to come."

Their mom's jaw tensed, and Claire sensed a coming storm. She held out her hands. "If you come with me, I'll get you some free snack vouchers. Will that help?"

All the kids perked up at 'snacks,' while she got the parents with 'free.' Contentment resurfaced as they headed out of the queue. Jack caught Claire by the arm.

"You're going to run us bankrupt if you keep giving food away," he said. Despite his words, his tone was gentle. "You're exactly like your dad. Always putting the guests first."

"Thanks, Jack," she replied, patting his hand. "That means a lot."

"Meet me back at the office in twenty?"

Chapter Two: Claire

"See you there!"

Thirty minutes later, Claire plopped into a chair opposite Jack's desk. "I had a minor crisis with a five-year-old and spilled ice cream."

"Free replacement?" Jack asked with a sigh.

"Yep."

"As I said. All right, Claire. I talked it over with maintenance, and it looks like Harvey will be out at least a week."

"A week!" she cried, her lacquered nails gripping her chair's armrests. "That means we're down two rides, and it's peak tourist season. If this keeps up..."

"Calm down," he replied. "We've weathered storms before. We'll redirect guests to the open rides and keep things moving."

"And if another ride breaks down?"

"We amp up interest in what's available." He whooshed out a breath. "And give out more vouchers, if necessary."

Claire listened to the steady beat of the wall clock, her heart straining to hear the soothing hum of the ocean. She opened her eyes to find Jack staring dreamily at a recent photo of him and Natalie, his arm slung around her shoulders, both smiling carefree at the camera.

"Mom said she enjoyed your date to Charleston last weekend."

"She did?" he asked, turning pink. "Your mom is something else. Man, I love that woman." He huffed out a laugh. "Who knew that after your dad and my wife died, Nat and I would find romance?"

"I'm very happy for y'all," she replied, letting his delight warm her through. "She's a strong woman, but I hated seeing her left alone."

Jack's brow wrinkled as he leaned his forearms on his desk. "Are you sure you don't mind? It can't be easy seeing your mom with another man."

"Maybe with 'another' man, Jack. You were already part of the family."

The corner of his mouth tipped up, sparking untold curiosity in Claire. Her mom and Jack had been dating for over a year. Wasn't it about time for him to pop the question? She swallowed the sudden lump in her throat.

While what she'd said to Jack was true, once they got past the cake tastings and wedding bells, Claire would no longer have her mom to herself. A man, albeit a great one, would be permanently in their lives. Popping over for a quiet dinner for two would be nigh on impossible, and Claire refused to think about what she might encounter if she forgot to call first.

"O-kay," she said aloud. "I'd better get back out there. See you later, Jack."

"Bye, kid!"

Outside, she made a beeline for the nearest ocean overlook. Breathing in the salty air always helped recenter her, giving a moment to reflect and pray. Once calm, she circled away from the Seagull Scrambler and soon found herself in front of the Widow's Walk, the park's haunted house boat ride. A teenaged couple, hand in hand, passed under the archway and into the cool darkness. Claire suspected they wouldn't exit without a few stolen kisses.

Memories of her teenage crush, the 'hunky and delicious' – *humph* – one-year-older Ryan Lanier, brought a familiar ache. He'd asked her to meet him out front of the Widow's Walk 'for one last ride' during his graduation party, but he never showed up. Ryan wasn't the prankster type, but he never explained his absence. Instead, he applied for a summer job in Knoxville before starting his freshman year at the University of Tennessee, and she'd rarely seen him since. She didn't want to believe a former friend's claims – that she told Ryan about nerdy Claire's crush and he bolted – but it was as good an explanation as any. He sure hadn't done anything to refute it.

She smoothed her hand over her platinum blonde locks and straightened her shoulders. While it wasn't what she was 'going for' with her vintage look, she knew she turned the heads of handsome, single men

Chapter Two: Claire

every now and then – the ones who preferred their women with a touch of class – at least, that's what she hoped. Seamed stockings were a tough look to pull off without looking like a pin-up girl.

"Ryan Lanier," she muttered, turning on her heels, "eat your heart... ouch!" *Who put that lamppost there?*

Ding, ding! As she pulled out her phone, she rubbed her shoulder. *Hopefully, no one saw that...*

"Oh no!"

Natalie: Mr. Lanier had another heart attack. He didn't make it. I'm meeting Helene at the hospital. Travis and Kendra are on their way.

Claire: I'll get Jack, and we'll meet you there.

As Claire shot her boss a text and hurried to meet him, another thought occurred to her. Ryan would return for the funeral.

"And then, he'll head back to Nashville...where he belongs."

But the thought of being around him again after all these years tightened her gut. She would have to give her condolences, but little more would need to pass between them. Travis would be the heir, after all. Ryan could ride off into the sunset...again.

Chapter Three: Ryan

Nashville, Tennessee

"The client wants what the client wants," the well-tailored woman said, her four-inch stilettos tapping through the concrete loft like claws in a dragon's lair. She swept her hand toward the breathtaking skyline view of downtown Nashville. "And this isn't it."

"Ms. Ross, as I've already mentioned," Ryan Lanier replied, swallowing his frustration, "your client's budget doesn't reach the amount they're asking downtown. Renovated factories on the outskirts are no less desirable, but the price is much lower." He stepped toward her, keeping his eyes on hers. Did she believe her mini skirt and low-cut blouse would work miracles? *Sheesh.*

As a junior commercial real estate broker at Nashboro-Montgomery, he wasn't permitted to scout those coveted properties. His district was well out of downtown, amongst the up-and-coming neighborhoods being renovated by people with big ideas and low budgets. While they were high-quality renos, they weren't Batman building height. More

Chapter Three: Ryan

like the R2-D2, formally known as One Nashville Place.

"Mr. Lanier," she said, resting her orange lacquered nails on his blue silk tie, "I expected more from Nashboro-Montgomery. I'm sure if you re-checked the listings," her fingers trailed to the tablet clenched against his chest, "you would find something more suitable."

Ding, ding! Saved by the text. Ryan retreated and whipped out his phone. *Three missed calls?*

Travis: Call me ASAP!

Ryan slipped it back into his pocket. He'd call once this meeting was concluded. Hardening his jaw, he pinned the agent with a stern glare that he hoped rivaled Mr. Wakowski in high school chemistry.

"I believe we're wasting our time here. Once I'm back at the office, I'll go over the listings again and speak with my supervisors." His broad shoulders, once toned by football, ached with stress, but he refused to show any sign of weakness. "Will that suffice?"

Her feral grin showed all of her bleached white teeth along with a broad band of pink gumline. He held back a shudder.

"It's almost dinnertime. Perhaps we could look together over…"

Ding, ding! Ryan strode away, pulling out his cell at a safe distance. Even if this time it was spam, he would do anything to avoid that woman's clutches.

Travis: Call me NOW!

"I'm sorry, Ms. Ross. I've received an urgent message. We'll have to postpone any further discussion." Like a kindergarten teacher in a sudden rainstorm, he herded her out of the loft, locked up, and hurried to his car. He watched her drive off before dialing Travis. His brother picked up immediately.

"What's up, Trav? I was with a client."

Instead of the teasing he expected, his brother's tone was grim. "It's Dad. He had another heart attack," Travis's breath caught, "and he didn't make it."

"What?" Ryan whispered, his air sucked out as by a vacuum.

"I know."

"Mom?"

"Better than expected, but man, you need to get here."

Ryan heard the hospital intercom and Kendra's soft nudgings. "I'll call the office and head out. Give Mom my love."

Ryan tossed his phone in the passenger seat and leaned his head back. *Dad is gone?* But he was finally taking some time off, taking it easy. Ryan punched the steering wheel. *That was supposed to prolong his life!*

"Why? It wasn't his time to die! Shoot, I wasn't ready for him to die."

The scene before him blurred, and being alone, Ryan gave in to the tears. If he didn't, he wasn't sure he'd make it safely to Pony Island. Whoever said real men don't cry obviously never met one.

After the first attack, the doctor told them to expect another, that it would most likely be fatal. Ryan spent a week afterward with his family, listening to his dad's awful jokes with a prayer in his heart.

"Son, I've lived a good life. I'm ready when my time comes. What I want for you is to move forward. Find a good woman, and don't let her go."

Ryan's earthly comfort came in the fact he'd been able to say *goodbye*.

* * *

Pony Island, the next day...

Ryan sat at the kitchen island, numbly watching Kendra make sandwiches for lunch. He'd driven through the night and crashed in his old room, waking an hour ago. He was irritated that no one woke him to go with his mom to the funeral home, but she insisted they had everything under control.

"You're not as young as you used to be, Ryan," she reminded him

Chapter Three: Ryan

on the phone. "You needed your rest, and Travis was able to join me. Come with Kendra after lunch."

His sister-in-law saw right through him. "Don't beat yourself up, Ryan. Your dad didn't want you to put your life on hold for him."

"But I should've come home more often. I know that. The park was too much of a stressor on Dad." He hung his head. "Maybe if I had stayed..."

"Ryan, really. Your parents were proud of your decision to forge your own path. They never begrudged you."

"I know, but..."

"No buts." She bagged up the last hoagie and shoved the pile toward him. "Now get *your butt* off that stool and put these in a shopping bag."

Pony Island had changed very little since he graduated high school, the small town dishing out its lazy coastal vibe to tourists in the summer and locals the rest of the year. He'd be lying if he said he didn't miss it sometimes in the midst of hustling Music City. As he walked beside Kendra, taking in the familiar sights, the Sand Dollar Ferris Wheel caught his eye.

Claire. His first crush. Though he'd hardly seen her since leaving for college, cherished memories flashed like his parents' old home movies – a little grainy and yellowed but no less precious.

For the past ten years, she'd never been around much when he visited his family...and he hadn't sought her out. She was probably avoiding him after he stood her up. That is, if she even showed. He had his doubts.

"Claire!" Kendra called, waving her toned arm. "Look who's here!"

Ryan's body kept moving even as his brain function died. *Claire here? Right now? Why now?* Oh, his dad. Blinking, he focused on the vision of a woman now standing in front of him, her expression guarded. Light blonde waves cascaded past her ivory cheek before swooping up into a classy updo. Familiar sky-blue eyes framed with long black lashes returned the examination.

"Ryan, I'm so sorry for your loss."

The words drew him to her bold red lips, totally unlike the Claire he remembered but oh-so…*Stop it, Lanier. She is way out of bounds.* After the quick pep talk, his brain returned to the field.

"Er, thank you. It's been a while, Claire. You're looking well."

"Thank you. You too." She lifted the shoulder of her black cocktail dress, making the white carnation pinned there wobble. "Kendra, how can I help?"

His sister-in-law unhooked the bag from his hand and prepared to slink off. "I'd better get these to the kitchen. You two catch up."

When he turned back to Claire, she was frowning. Without a backward glance, she started off. He followed at a jog.

"I was headed to the funeral home," she explained. "My mom's there."

"Mine too." *Obviously, dude.* "So, how've you been?"

"Good. Great. Except for your father's passing. He will be missed." He was surprised she could hoof it in those black pumps. Even his pulse was erratic…or maybe it wasn't the speed-walking. "How are you, otherwise?"

"Not too bad. I was working with a client when Travis called." *A client, huh. Ms. Ross was more like a piranha.* Why did he bring her up? He took the moment of silence to take Claire in properly. When did she get so…vintage? Despite himself, the side of his mouth lifted. Cute and classy. *I like it…WHOA! Not going there.*

"Nashville's treating you well, then?" Claire asked, casting him a sweeping once-over before turning pink. *Is she checking me out?* Of its own accord, his chest puffed.

"I guess you could say that." They reached the front door of the funeral home. "I'm sorry I didn't make it back for your father's funeral. I was out of the country."

Claire whirled on him, her back to the glass door, and her smile,

Chapter Three: Ryan

forced. "Don't worry about it. I'm happy things are working out for you. I'd better go find my mother. Will I see you around...other than?" She pointed behind her.

"Maybe. I'll be here for a few days."

"Cool. Right. Bye."

He held the door for her as she disappeared into the cold sanctuary. Claire Hensley. Yep. *I'm still interested.* Pity it would never work. His life was in Nashville, and someday they'd pry her cold, dead hands off Pony Island. Claire wasn't going anywhere willingly.

* * *

The day of the funeral passed in a black blur. Ryan barely saw Claire as she insisted on handling the food and the needs of the family. Her mom Natalie stayed by his mom's side, lending her experience and strength to her best friend.

The next day dawned in a drizzle. Ryan found his mom curled up on the sofa, a cold cup of coffee in her hands, forgotten.

"I can't believe he's gone," she whispered as he sat next to her. She wiped away a tear. "That sounds cliché, doesn't it?"

"No, Mom, not at all." He took her hand in his, moving her cup to the coffee table. "Because it's been said a million times, doesn't make it any less true."

"When did you get so wise?" she asked, cupping his dark beard. "You look more and more like your father every time I see you. Oh, my boy. I've missed you."

"I've missed you too, Mom. I know I should have..."

"Hush, Ryan. You're here now." She picked up a family photo taken in front of the gates of the park, touching her finger to his father's smiling face. "We have a meeting with Mr. Dunlap at one to discuss the inheritance."

"I assumed everything went to you."

"All of our personal property does, but there's still the matter of the park. Like Natalie, I have no desire to handle the running of it."

"Travis, then, I assume." Ryan released her hand to put both of his behind his head. The stretch popped several tight spots. *That's the stuff.*

"No, not Travis."

"Huh?" What was she talking about? His brother worked at the park. He was the obvious choice.

"We talked to Travis and Kendra a year ago, but they declined ownership."

"But why?"

"I honestly don't know, but I suspect they need their family time," Helene said, visions of grandchildren dancing in her head. Ryan groaned.

"Who, then? Is Jack buying you out?"

"No. He's fixin' to retire. He and Natalie want to travel."

The tightness in his shoulders moved to his gut. "Are you selling?"

"That's not my plan, no." She pulled his chin toward her. "Ryan, you're the heir, and we all trust you to do the right thing."

"The right thing? Mom, I live in Nashville. I have a job, friends, responsibilities. I can't drop everything…"

"I know that, baby. No one is asking you to move." After patting his hand, she pushed to her feet. "The truth is, the future of the park is in question. We're hoping that with your business sense and Claire's connection to the area, you two will come up with a viable solution."

"You're asking me to save a *dying* amusement park?"

Chapter Four: Ryan

Helene paused by a photo of his dad on the mantle. "No. I'm asking you to assess the situation and decide with Claire what is best for everyone."

He let out a whistle. "That's a tall order, Mom. Claire will likely kill me if we have to close."

"Maybe." She winked. "Or perhaps that crush of yours will finally come to fruition. She's single, you know."

"Mom! Seriously? That was ages ago."

"Son, you'd have to be blind not to see what a beauty our Claire has become, and with a heart as good as gold! Now, I'm off to take a shower. If anyone calls, take a message."

As his mom hoped, Ryan's thoughts drifted to his high school crush all-grown-up. He wasn't surprised his mom sussed out his past feelings, but to insinuate he had a hope now? *Fat chance.* He pushed himself up, determined to put this park business behind him and Claire Hensley out of his heart.

* * *

Numbers don't lie, Ryan reminded himself, dreading the upcoming meeting. He'd gone over the park's finances from stem to stern. Without a serious influx of cash, the Pony Island Amusement Park would soon flounder. All of the money was accounted for, which was a huge relief. He hadn't suspected anything amiss, but it was nice to know their people could be trusted. Now, he needed to figure out what made Claire tick.

They would have to sell. There was no other option. Ticket sales were way down, vacationers preferring the upscale amenities of other islands. And the discount for locals? They were practically paying them to visit. No, unless God sent a miracle, the Pony Island Amusement Park was in its last season.

His chest grew tight at the thought. This was their grandparents' dream. After World War II, the country was craving lighthearted, family-friendly entertainment. The 1950s dawned in Postwar prosperity, and vacation travel boomed. From then until the 1990s, Pony Island had steadily grown. At the turn of the century, though, when Ryan and Claire were in elementary school, the world changed. People began to seek gratification in the new and different. Nostalgia became a way of the past.

It's time to put the Pony Island Amusement Park out to pasture.

Ryan and his mother arrived at Mr. Dunlap's office a few minutes early and were shown into a meeting room. A familiar face sat in one of the chairs, scanning her phone. When she heard them enter, Claire's head popped up.

"Ryan? What are you doing here?" Scrambling to her feet, she pulled his mom into a hug. "Helene, how are you doing? Is there anything I can do?"

"As well as can be expected," Helene replied. "No. I'm being well taken care of. Smothered, actually."

"Mom..."

Chapter Four: Ryan

She tugged him forward, sending Claire teetering back on her heels searching for an escape. "Please, take him off my hands."

"Wait. Aren't you staying for the meeting?" he asked, divided between his mom's slinking to the door and Claire's edging to the far side of the table.

"No, dear. I came to sign a few papers. Once that's over with, I'm going to visit Natalie."

"Oh." Ryan returned her wave halfheartedly. Mr. Dunlap saved him from making small talk with Claire.

"Good. You're both here," the aging lawyer said, placing three folders on the table. "Please, Ryan, have a seat."

Claire tracked him all the way. When he met her straight on, she stiffened.

"I was expecting Travis."

"So was I," he replied, a low growl betraying his irritation. His brother worked at the park. He knew it better than Ryan. Why had he passed on ownership? "But you've got me instead. Now, Mr. Dunlap, why don't you tell us what this meeting is about."

"Spoken like a true businessman." The lawyer tented his fingers. "I asked you here today to deal first with the transfer of ownership, and second, to make you both aware of the park's full situation."

"Its full situation?" Claire repeated. "What do you mean?"

Mr. Dunlap slid a document toward Ryan. "Please read this transfer and sign below. We'll get to that in a moment, Claire."

"Wait. It says here," Ryan said, "that I'm receiving 45% of the park. This must be a typo."

"No," the lawyer said, sighing. "It's not a typo."

"Then, I own 55%?" Claire asked. "I don't remember that."

"No. You each own 45%."

"Who owns the other 10%?" Ryan asked, sharing Claire's bafflement.

"That's what I asked you here to discuss, but I can't do so until you are signed as co-owner."

"Fine." Ryan read the document again before scrawling his signature. He tossed the pen on the table. "Explain."

After placing the page in a manila folder, Mr. Dunlap returned to his tented position. "As you know, your grandparents were the original co-owners of the Pony Island Amusement Park. After their deaths, the park passed to your fathers. Now, you two are the owners."

"Yes, sir. We know all that," Claire said politely, but Ryan detected hints of their shared frustration.

"Patience, my dear. It is in a lawyer's best interest to lay out all of the facts. Now, where were we?"

"We're the owners now," Ryan replied.

"Right. You two own the park together, but there is a third party. When your grandparents developed the property, they felt it best to split the investment between three entities rather than two, in case of future squabbles. Most of the time, the Pony Island Corporation, or PIC, is happy to remain in the background, but with the park's recent financial troubles, they came to me with an ultimatum to present to you."

"An ultimatum?" Claire cried. "What kind of ultimatum? Do they want us to close the park?"

Mr. Dunlap shook his head. "Let's not be hasty. They have not shared their opinion either way."

"Who is the Pony Island Corporation? Why have we never heard of them?" Ryan asked, leaning forward. "Why aren't they at this meeting?"

"They wish to remain anonymous for the time being."

Afternoon sunlight streamed through the blinds as Claire and Ryan peppered the lawyer with questions. He held up his hands to silence them.

"I'm sorry, but I cannot reveal their identity. However, I believe you will find that it doesn't matter." He gestured to their closed folders.

Chapter Four: Ryan

"Please look inside."

Ryan pulled out a typed, notarized letter dated two days prior. It stated that the Pony Island Corporation would not interfere with the decisions of the other two owners except in regards to the question of the property's sale. Before they would agree to sell, Claire and Ryan must complete a full evaluation of the entire park, including riding all of the rides together.

"I refuse to sell," Claire stated, pinning him with a glare, "so that's that."

"But selling may be our only option," Ryan replied, revealing his position. Her lips thinned to almost nothing.

"Read on," Mr. Dunlap said.

If, on the other hand, they believed the park could be saved, the PIC would match whatever funds they invested for repairs – up to an undisclosed amount. Claire's face lit up with a dazzling smile.

"That's our solution, then. We save the money for repairs, restore the park, and Ryan, you can go back to Nashville."

He refused to give in. "What's my 45% worth, Mr. Dunlap?"

Claire's sharp inhale struck him like a knife in the heart. "You would consider selling me out?"

"Selling you out?"

"Leaving me in the hands of some unknown." She threw up her hands. "What if they wanted to change the park? Turn it into something awful, like a…a…surf club?"

"A surf club?" he replied, his mouth twitching. "What would surfers want with a bunch of derelict amusement park rides?"

"Derelict? Why you…"

"Claire, Ryan," Mr. Dunlap interjected. "This is neither the time nor place…"

Claire rose to her feet, and before he could help himself, Ryan absorbed the graceful lines of her hourglass figure. *Am I really suggesting leaving Claire in the lurch?* His lunch burger turned to a rock, but before he could amend his position, she poked her blood-red nail in his direction.

"You hear me right now, Ryan Lanier! I'm not losing my beloved park without a fight. Pony Island is more than my home; it's in my blood. If you take that away, you might as well kill me too. Good day, Mr. Dunlap."

As she stormed off in a swish of navy skirts and red heels, Ryan propped his chin in his hand. Claire Hensley was still a firecracker. He would have to be on his guard.

Chapter Five: Claire

Trading her ruby pumps for practical tennies, Claire hopped on her light blue cruiser bicycle and sped out of the parking lot, fuming. Even though she'd obtained a driver's license, Claire rarely rode in a car. Few people on the island owned them, preferring golf carts and bicycles. Ryan probably had some fancy car, one that parked itself and had sensors that deprived the driver of common sense.

How dare he come all the way from Nashville, Tennessee to her Palmetto State island and have the nerve to suggest *she* should sell the park! *What does he know about it? He's never here!* If he took the time to visit every now and then, he would see how excited Meredith Hatfield was at her Five Star-fish birthday party or witness the thrill of the park's Easter Egg-stravagan-Sea!

"If the sight of little kids wearing Sea-Horse headbands and hunting chocolate shells wouldn't sway him, he would be past saving," she muttered, her breathing labored more from heartbreak than exertion. If her gut twisted up any more, it would be a soft pretzel.

Who was behind the Pony Island Corporation, and why had no one ever mentioned it? Surely their parents knew. She texted her mother.

Seconds later, Natalie replied.

Natalie: No, I've never heard of them. Your father never mentioned them either, so I doubt he knew.

Claire: OK. Thanks, Mom.

Natalie: How did the meeting go otherwise? How was Ryan?

Claire: Awful. We'll talk later.

Her mother's question tumbled like a pebble underwater through her mind. *How was Ryan?* Other than being an obnoxious jerk, he was still the handsomest guy ever. *And now, I have a thing for beards.*

The road swung down the cape to her home, a fully-restored lighthouse – minus the light. It was her childhood home, but after her father died, Natalie moved into a cottage in town. Claire didn't mind the isolation. It was nice to have space after days at the park, and she enjoyed the daily bike rides. The downside was the rainy days, but even then, she could stoke up a warm fire in the keeper's cottage's pellet stove.

The navy and white spirals of the light tower beckoned. At the top under the bright red turret roof was the highest spot on the island and Claire's reading loft. The light was removed when, in the 1980s, the coast guard built a new electric lighthouse on a different beach. The balcony around the top was now the perfect spot for after-dinner coffee or an early morning tea. Below the curved windows, Claire kept rows of her favorite volumes – mysteries, romances, and the classics. Up in her happy place, she was never without companionship.

Ryan, Travis, and Kendra visited the tower often growing up. For the longest time, Claire harbored a secret fantasy of being kissed as the sun set over the mainland. When she finally had her first kiss, it wasn't Ryan nor at the top of the lighthouse. The boy in question was long gone from the island, and she would be content if he never returned.

But Ryan's back, her heart reminded her, as if she'd forgotten. *Man, he looks incredible. He must work out.*

Chapter Five: Claire

And if his clothes weren't custom tailored, she'd eat her straw boater. The way the crisp cotton of his dress shirt rounded over his broad shoulders and around his strong arms...what she wouldn't give to be in those arms, snug and safe. Her Hollywood crushes, the incomparable Cary Grant and Jimmy Stewart, paled in comparison.

"Snap out of it, Claire!" she reprimanded. She did not need these mental pictures. As long as he advocated selling the park, Ryan Lanier was her enemy. "Even if he dons a fedora and whisks me off to Niagara Falls!"

Past the lighthouse, the road dipped down and around to the beach and the island's nature reserve. A herd of wild ponies, descended from a few left behind by Spanish explorers in the 1500s, roamed free. These were where Pony Island got its name. It had nothing to do with Coney Island. *Nothing whatsoever.*

Usually, the sight of the ponies leisurely grazing, the fresh scent of the ocean, and the gnarled live oaks, their Spanish moss swaying in the breeze, settled her nerves and cleared her head, but not today. She stopped under a tree as a painted chestnut foal wandered into the road ahead, curious but too cautious to approach. Interacting with the ponies was strictly forbidden by all but the nature conservation, of which Claire was not a part. After a good long-distance sniff, the foal passed on. As Claire started off, she felt a tug on her waistline.

"Shoot!"

She was so distracted that her skirt got caught in the chain. She gently removed it and assessed the damage. The metal tore a small hole in the thick crepe, and it was stained with chain oil. *Great.*

"You owe me a new skirt, Ryan Lanier! This is all your fault!"

The foal's mama whinnied as if to tell Claire to *shush*, and she headed on, repentant...to the ponies, not Ryan. It was her way to 'make do and mend,' but from now on, this skirt would be tainted by the likes of the Islander-turned-City-Boy. Maybe she should throw it away.

***

After her ride, Claire spent the rest of the day in the office. Around six o'clock, her phone dinged.

Unknown Number: Hey, Claire. It's Ryan. Will you have lunch with me tomorrow? We need to talk.

Travis must have given him her number.

Claire: What's there to talk about? You've already made up your mind.

Rains: I still think we need to talk. We're co-owners, after all.

Claire: Fine. Meet me at Piper's at noon. Don't be late.

Lugosi: *thumbs up*

"What's wrong?" Kendra asked, pulling Claire from her internal debate over which actor was the best choice for Ryan's number. It was hardly fair to compare either the Invisible Man or Dracula to Ryan Lanier, although all three were villains. She was sure both Dr. Jack Griffin and the Count would vote to save the park.

"Everything." After making sure no one else was around, Claire confided her fears. "Ryan wants to sell, and I'm afraid he may be right."

"Are you giving up already?"

"No! And don't you dare tell him or Travis I admitted that. I did some thinking after our meeting, and as much as it kills me, I don't have any ideas left. I feel like we've tried everything."

Kendra ran out to the vending machine and brought back two candy bars. Claire bit into the chocolate, nougat, and almonds with a groan before launching into an abbreviated account of the meeting, minus the ogling bits.

"He asked to meet with me tomorrow," Claire said, sticking her thumb to her chest. "I may be frantic and heartbroken in here, but he'll never know. My optimism will know no bounds."

Kendra patted her on the shoulder. "Honey, you wear your heart on

Chapter Five: Claire

your sleeve, and Ryan's no idiot. He's going to know you're at wits' end."

"Then, he can also know I'll do anything to save this park." Her enthusiasm drew both girls to their feet for a double high-five.

"You go, girl!" Kendra said. "I..." *Ding, ding!* After she looked at the screen, she pressed it to her chest. "Sorry, Claire, but I need to make a call." Before Claire could respond, her best friend was out of sight, leaving her alone in the office.

Plopping back into her swivel chair, Claire drifted to the photos on her walls. Some were from the park's 1949 opening, the grandparents smiling, untroubled. Others showed the park in various stages of construction and renovation.

Her favorites, though, were the snapshots of family and friends enjoying the little oasis. There were even a few of Ryan, either squinting into the sun or posing like the goofy kid she'd fallen for. Mr. Lanier's ever-present smile warmed her heart. While they had never been close, Ryan's dad was someone she knew she could count on. *What would he think about Ryan's push to sell?* She couldn't imagine he'd be too thrilled, the park being as much his home as hers.

Nostalgia.

Like a new day, it dawned on her. *If I can make Ryan remember how much fun he used to have at the park, surely, he'll see the need to keep it open!* From there, her wheels started turning. She grabbed a notepad.

"What Ryan doesn't realize," she told the empty room, "is that vintage is making a comeback. If we can find the people who appreciate it and who will support us, we can get Pony Island back on the map!"

And then, she saw the chocolate thumbprint on her blouse.

"Seriously? That man has turned me into a total klutz!"

* * *

Claire's burst of enthusiasm didn't wake up with her the next morning. All she accomplished was a series of doodles, mostly swirls and polka dots. After watering her raised vegetable garden and fixing a salad full of homegrown goodness, she trawled the internet late into the night, searching for clubs of vintage enthusiasts who were close enough to entice to the park. The list totaled zero.

"Back to square one," she said, striding out into the park. After putting on her round light blue sunglasses, a favorite in her collection, she spotted Morgan Sullivan, one of their summer interns, manning a nearby popcorn stand.

"Good morning, Claire," the pretty teen said, her braces glinting in the bright sunlight. "You always look so cute. You should totally start a vintage fashion blog or something."

"Goodness, no!" Claire replied. "For one, I wouldn't know the first thing about blogging, and second, I highly doubt there are that many people who would be interested."

"Oh, come on! It would be fun!" Morgan danced on her toes. "If you didn't want a full blog, you could do social media. Snap a few pictures and write a caption. Easy!"

"No, not easy! And you know I don't do social media. Everyone sharing everything about their lives all over the internet?" Claire cringed. "That's not me."

"But you don't have to share everything," the girl protested. "Only the things you want to share. It would be great publicity for the park."

She knew Claire's weakness, but *her* on social media? She'd been down that road years ago when it was first popular. Now that she was free of its clutches, did she want to return? Nope. Plus, they barely had any website traffic. Why would social media be any different?

"Thanks for the idea, Morgan," she replied, "but I'm going to pass for now."

"OK. Want some popcorn?"

Chapter Five: Claire

"No, thanks," Claire replied, inhaling the addictive scent, "but it sure smells good."

"Freshly made." Morgan scooped out a small cupful and passed it over. "Go on. You look like you need it."

"If you insist." As soon as she popped a puff into her mouth, her taste buds danced in delight. Maybe she *had* needed it. "How's business?"

"Well...not too many people want popcorn at nine in the morning." Something hovered behind the girl's comment. Claire waved her on. "I hope you don't mind, but I've been thinking. What if we waited to open the popcorn stands until eleven? That way, we'd have less waste..."

"Excuse me," a burly guest said from behind Claire. "How much is your biggest bucket?"

Morgan turned beet pink, her embarrassment leaking into her ginger hair.

"Don't worry," Claire reassured her. "We'll talk more later. I want to hear your ideas."

Relief flooded the teen before she turned to fix the guest's order. While Morgan was right about the waste, morning popcorn was a die-hard tradition for some guests. Claire wasn't sure spoiling traditions was the way to rebuild their customer base.

Jacob Hampton, the aforementioned wearer of the Sea-Horse suit, passed Claire with a wave, his attention drawn over her shoulder to Morgan. His longing cut Claire to the quick. The cute but nerdy boy had it bad. How his crush felt, Claire had no idea. It was against her personal policy to interfere in the love lives of others. She'd had her heart broken by a meddler, and she refused to cause another young soul the same pain.

Chapter Six: Ryan

"Selling is our best option."

Ryan's mom exchanged a look with Travis. "We understand where you're coming from, we do, but…"

"But what? I've run the numbers, and if the park's fortunes keep going as they are, you're going to run out of money."

Travis cleared his throat. "Don't you mean, *we're* going to run out of money? It's your park too now."

The back of Ryan's neck grew hot. "I know that. I'm not used to the idea yet."

Helene fidgeted with the napkin in her hands. "Life's not all about money, darling. Although our numbers are down, we're one of the few family-owned amusement parks left in the country. We have regulars coming in from as far as Oklahoma."

"That's hardly something to write home about, Mom."

"No, but the point is, they do come. Every. Year." She pierced him with a glare. "If we close, where would they go?"

"Dollywood."

"Ryan!"

Travis waved his hand between them. "Stop it, you two. Ryan, if

Chapter Six: Ryan

they wanted to go to Dollywood, they wouldn't travel six hours farther, and Mom, Ryan is right. We can't keep the park open to cater to a few out-of-town regulars if we run out of money. What we need is a solid plan."

Ryan opened the browser on his laptop. "I've done my research. With the right presentation, we could attract the attention of a big-name amusement park operator. If they like what they see, they buy the park, make necessary changes, spend the thousands we don't have on advertising, and voila, the park's saved."

Helene scrolled through a few websites before resting her clasped hands on the table. "I know how these things work, Ryan. Big companies come in, strip all of the local personality out of a place, and replace it with cookie-cutter themes and crass entertainment. Then, Pony Island would be overrun with tourists expecting bars and nightlife, the local government would feel forced to give in, and life on the island as we know it would be gone."

"Not necessarily," he replied, pulling up the website of an amusement park in North Carolina. "That's not what happened here. See for yourself."

After looking over the photos, both Helene and Travis begrudged him a small victory. His mom rose from the table.

"You know I will support you no matter what you choose, but I ask one thing in return."

He had a feeling he knew. "What, Mom?"

"Before you set your mind on anything, work with Claire."

"I am working with Claire. We're meeting in, oh, an hour at Piper's."

"No, Ryan," Helene said, leaning down to his level, "you're not. You've already decided. Pony Island means the world to that girl. No, let me speak. Claire is an intelligent young woman. If selling is the only viable option, she will do the right thing. However, as long as hope remains, stay open to her ideas and thoughts. Co-owning a business is like a marriage. You have to compromise, give and take."

The thought of any kind of marriage to Claire, even a business one, fired up his senses.

"I knew it! You still like her!" Travis pumped his arm before fist-bumping his mom. "Shut down the park, lose the girl. It's that simple, dude."

Even half an hour later, as Ryan strode uneasily toward the restaurant, he couldn't help musing over whether the opposite was true. *Save the park, get the girl? Could it be that simple?*

* * *

"My position hasn't changed," Claire declared upon arrival. Her storm cloud turned into pure sunshine as she addressed the waitress. "Allie, how are you doing? Is the summer quarter still a bear?"

"It sure is," the college-aged girl replied. "What can I get y'all?"

Playing the gentleman, he deferred to Claire.

"I'll have sweet tea and crab salad."

Ryan opted for a shrimp po-boy and fries. Claire gave Allie's arm a squeeze before returning stiffly to him.

Piper's Restaurant, rebuilt after a hurricane in the early 1970s, resembled a wood-sided beach house painted in a vibrant aqua, now peeling, with doors for windows and tall teal shutters. Worn white rocking chairs beckoned from the wraparound porch, tempting visitors with a peaceful respite from the heat of the day.

The dining room was open to allow the breeze to blow through, aided by huge woven fans hanging from the fifteen-foot ceilings. The décor was unchanged – faded prints of palm leaves and pink hibiscus paired with woven woods and bamboo. It was a dated look that either endeared visitors or turned them off, in Ryan's opinion.

Over seventy years old, the surrounding tropical garden was lush and

Chapter Six: Ryan

green, brimming with saw palmettos, mandevillas, birds of paradise, and the occasional Japanese lantern. Their table on the fringe of the outdoor dining area, with a view of the Atlantic surf framed by sabal palmettos, was more of a date spot than a battlefield.

"I'm not the bad guy here," he said. "I want what's best for the park."

"And how in blue blazes would you know what that is?" she hissed, casing the clientele and finding them isolated. "How many times have you been back? Three? Four?"

"That's not fair, Claire. I have a job in Nashville. Responsibilities. I can't run home whenever I feel like it."

"People make time for what's most important, Ryan," she replied.

Allie brought their drinks while her true comment hung in the air. He debated various responses but settled, for some reason, on,

"You missed me." Her plump red lips formed an 'O', and he leaned forward. "That's what I'm hearing, anyway."

When Claire crossed her tanned arms over the front of her lemon-yellow sundress, he noticed a faint rosiness on her neck. She broke eye contact to fiddle with the sunglasses holding back her light blonde hair. Her nails were still red. Red nail polish, red lipstick. *Why red? What am I missing here?*

"Not at all. Why would I?"

Her harsh tone shot him down to earth. "No reason. Let's stick to business, huh?"

"Fine."

He was used to pushing for quick sales and calling the shots. His tried-and-true method involved laying out his strongest case and negotiating the details.

"Fine. Here's why I believe selling the park is the best option: one, we're barely making a profit. Two, the rides need a very expensive overhaul. Three…"

"I know all of this," Claire replied. When their food promptly arrived, she didn't touch hers. Ryan bit into a fry as encouragement. Maybe if he could get her to relax and eat, she would be more willing to listen. "Let me make my position abundantly clear. I refuse...do you hear me, Ryan? I *refuse* to sell until we've exhausted all other avenues. Period."

"Then you acknowledge the possibility?"

"I acknowledge nothing, and until that time comes, I'm not going to discuss it."

"You're bailing water out of a sinking ship!" He shoved a fry into the house dip. As flavor exploded in his mouth, he held back a groan. He'd forgotten how amazing Pony Island fry sauce was.

"A *sinking* ship?" she shrieked, scaring off a seagull poaching two tables away. "There are other options we haven't even discussed. What about the PIC's offer to match funds? Isn't that worth a try?"

Chapter Seven: Ryan

Worth a try. Huh. That's what he told himself before his graduation party, and look how that turned out. Old feelings bubbled to the surface in the silence. Claire picked at her food while his memories ran wild.

Young Ryan finally worked up the nerve. He was going to ask Claire out during his party. He slipped her a note asking her to meet him in front of the Widow's Walk at nine. At 8:36, one of her friends pulled him aside.

"Claire's madly in love with Kyle Merritt. She wants you to tell him."

"I'm not telling him anything," Ryan retorted, his adolescent heart breaking. "She can tell him herself."

"But she doesn't know if he likes her."

Ryan knew for a fact he and Kyle harbored crushes on the same girl, although it was never discussed. But Claire crushing on Kyle? That didn't make any sense. Ryan was pretty confident she liked him, at least more than she liked his friend. But Lauren was her friend, so she must be telling the truth.

"Yeah, he likes her," he replied, sagging. "A lot."

Lauren's smile grew wider than the sound separating them from the mainland, and she rested her glittery nails on his chest.

"Thanks, Ryan. See you later?"

While he managed to avoid Lauren for the rest of the night, he would never forget the sight, a quarter of an hour later, of Claire laughing with Kyle by the refreshment table. If she made their rendezvous, he didn't know. He spent the rest of the night getting beat in *Gran Turismo* and left for college without seeing her.

Ryan regretted every moment of that decision, but he never worked up the nerve to call her. Why? For two simple reasons: teenaged boys don't take rejection well, and neither do they enjoy talking on the phone. Yeah, he could've texted. It was a thing, the 'multi-tap' method and all, but what would he have said?

Ryan: Hey! I ditched u bc Lauren said u like Kyle. Sry.

That would've gone over well. Even in plain speech, it would be mortifying.

Once upon a time, Ryan and Claire were fairly close. Never best friends, but growing up together brought its own bond. From diapers until graduation, their days intertwined until he couldn't imagine a life without her. Back then, with her sleek ponytail, jean shorts, and colorful t-shirts, she was the prettiest girl he knew. Feisty too. When Claire had an idea, it was bound to be fun. Ryan, on the other hand, was the one keeping the group from running off a cliff like lemmings. Even back then, he knew they balanced each other, and he'd let his teenage fantasies run rampant.

He peeked over his sandwich at the grown woman across from him, all shined and polished, and pushed those memories back into a drawer. His stubbornness killed their friendship, and the fact remained that he never tried to revive it. No wonder she was the ice queen.

"I asked," Claire repeated, stabbing a hunk of crab with her fork, "why you won't consider trying to save the money first? We'll be afloat for the rest of the season. This winter, while the park's closed, we can

Chapter Seven: Ryan

brainstorm."

"I won't be here this winter," he replied. "I live in Nashville, remember?"

"What does that matter? You don't have to be here. The rest of us can handle it."

"Like you've been handling it without me?"

The blue of her eyes raged like a stormy sea. "Why, you..."

"C'mon, Claire. We might not be in this mess if..."

Ice cold sweet tea streamed from his hair over his face and ears, shocking his system. His indignation fizzled upon the sight of the fire goddess before him.

"You arrogant, egotistical, unfeeling jerk! We were doing fine without you butting your nose in where it wasn't wanted. The sooner you leave, the better!" She stalked to the edge of the patio, spinning for one last parting shot. *"Dum spiro spero*, Ryan Lanier. *Dum spiro spero."*

The Latin needed no translation. It was drilled into them by their middle school history teacher, Mr. Knight. *Dum spiro spero* was South Carolina's state motto, meaning 'While I breathe, I hope.'

Claire Hensley wasn't going down without a fight. As the tea congealed in the heat, leaving him a sticky mess, he began to consider – for the first time – that he might be waging a losing battle. Was there any possible way to get through to her before he had to return to Nashville?

Ryan's job wasn't the only thing urging him back to Tennessee. Last night, his college friend Dominic called about Michael's March, their annual 5K run. Named for his brother, the foundation raised money for patients with multiple sclerosis as well as treatment centers and research groups. This time of the year, they were usually in the thick of planning, contacting past sponsors and seeking new ones. Ryan, with his head for numbers, was in charge of the event's budget. Outgoing Dominic excelled in the social side.

"I hate to rush you, man," Dominic said after asking how Ryan and his family were doing. "I know how important family time is."

"It's more than that," Ryan replied, the park's finances spread out on the bed. "Claire's determined to keep the park open, no matter the cost. She'll go down with this ship, for sure."

"And this is the same Claire you were pining over freshman year?"

"Old news, my friend." *I'm lying through my teeth.* "This is strictly business."

"Uh-huh, sure." Dominic's chuckle rumbled through the speaker. "You were never a good liar."

Time for a change of subject. "How are things on your end?"

"Real subtle. Okay, I'll bite. Michael had another flare-up yesterday, so I'm covering two jobs. Lacey's got her hands full with the kids, and Taylor's hours are already too long." He paused. "Suffice it to say, we're all stretched a little thin."

"You know I'd help if I could." Ryan sank back on his pillows. "I brought my laptop, so keep sending bills and receipts."

"You're a lifesaver, man. Don't know what we'd do without you."

* * *

"You look like you could use this," said a familiar voice. Ryan turned to find Miss Hattie with a damp rag in one hand and a slice of Pony Island Peach Cake in the other.

He inspected the dress shirt now plastered to his chest. "Thank you, ma'am, but I believe it's going to take more than that to get rid of this mess."

"You can say that again," she replied, sitting in Claire's abandoned chair while he tried to clean himself up. "I'm not sure what you said to her, but that girl sure skedaddled out of here."

"The simple explanation is she's too idealistic. Decisions in this

Chapter Seven: Ryan

business need to be quick and decisive. We don't have time to fool around, waiting on a miracle."

"I see. Are you referring to the future of the park?"

Ryan met Miss Hattie's impassive expression with squirrels in his stomach. That look meant she wasn't at all happy with him.

"Yes, ma'am. Believe me, I want to save it, but I ran the numbers, and there's no way it will work."

Her face didn't change. More squirrels. "I see."

"Do you?" he replied, his voice squeaking like a preteen. He cleared his throat, but she cut him off.

"I'm disappointed in you, Ryan Lanier. Didn't your parents raise you better than this?"

"What?"

She poked the table with her wrinkly finger. "The Ryan I knew wasn't a quitter."

"It's not being a quitter when you're following the evidence. Numbers don't lie, ma'am."

Her already stick straight back morphed into a general at war. "Numbers aren't everything, young man. People matter. Jobs matter. Hopes and dreams matter." She scooted the plate under his nose. "Eat this. I need to get back to the kitchen."

With a peck on the top of his head, his old friend scurried off. He scooped up a big bite of the cake, died, and went to dessert heaven. It was as amazing as he remembered.

Miss Hattie's specialty was a light yet decadent yellow sponge cake infused with house-made peach preserves. She topped the cake with fluffy peaches and cream frosting, sugared peaches, and a dusting of lemon sugar for a kick. Served with a hefty scoop of lemon sherbet, it was a Pony Island treasure.

The bite hit his stomach like a boulder. *Treasures are worth saving.*

Chapter Eight: Claire

"Oh my stars!" Claire cried, pressing her palms to her warm cheeks. "I did *not* just do that!"

As she slipped through the thin crowd near the Rolling Waves Coaster, she wasn't sure which was more mortifying: giving in physically to her anger or the sight of Ryan's wet shirt clinging to his toned pectorals. She did *not* need any more of that!

Stopping under a shade tree, she debated whether to text him an apology. She'd doused him with an entire glass of iced tea…because he wouldn't stop pushing that they sell. He wouldn't even listen to her ideas! What he deserved was a swift kick. She'd been too easy on him.

"I'm not going to apologize," she decided. "He should come crawling to me."

Ding, ding! That was probably Ryan now. Her ire cooled when she saw the text from Kendra.

Kendra: Morgan can't get the frozen drink machine working. Should I call maintenance, or do you want to handle it?

With the recent cuts, Claire tried to take care of as many minor hiccups herself as she could.

Claire: Tell her I'm on the way. Don't you dare let Travis tell Ryan

Chapter Eight: Claire

something else is broken.

Kendra: 10-4

When she reached the kiosk, Travis was already there. Claire rushed inside.

"What's wrong? Can we fix it?"

"You're the wizard here," he replied, bowing out. Morgan stood by, staring at the silent machine with a bit lip.

"Please don't tell your brother!" Claire called through the open door. "He'll add it to his list of reasons we must sell."

"I just work here!"

Shaking her head, Claire turned to Morgan. "What seems to be the problem?"

"It started freezing up." She pointed to the agitator blades. "The spiral things stopped spinning. I was afraid it would break, so I turned it off."

"Good thinking. Grab me a bucket."

While the girl did her bidding, Claire looked down at her yellow sundress. She would have to be careful. Positioning the bucket under the spigot, she asked Morgan to flip the power switch. The slush machine hummed to life, and the blades spun unhindered. After a few minutes, Claire turned to Morgan in relief.

"Looks like you fixed the…"

Drink mix exploded from the machine, showering Claire in Cherry-Berry Blast! Screaming, she dropped the bucket. Morgan caught her when her heel slipped on the slushy floor.

"Claire! Are you okay?"

"I'm fine," she replied, wobbling back to turn off the machine. "What on earth happened?"

Morgan wagged her head, wide-eyed and paying no heed to her new spray of cherry freckles. "I have no idea! Are you going to fire me?"

"Not unless you rigged it to do that."

"No!"

Claire almost patted the girl on the shoulder, but her hands were filthy. Morgan would have enough trouble getting her uniform clean without her boss adding to the mess.

"Better shut the window. We need to get this cleaned up."

For the next two hours, they hunted and scrubbed every speck of sticky red liquid. Claire made a mental note to add a little extra to Morgan's weekly wage.

"Other than this surprise bonding time with your boss, how do you like working here?" she asked, running her rag over a metal cabinet.

Morgan grinned as she refilled her cleaning bucket. "It's fun. Even this."

"Making any friends?"

"A few. Some of the other interns are going to the movies tomorrow and asked me to go."

"That sounds fun!" Claire expected her to elaborate, but Morgan grew silent. Was she thinking about someone in particular? "We've had many lasting friendships forged behind these gates. I hope that's true for you too."

"Thanks, Claire. Me too." If Claire was hoping Morgan would spill her feelings about a certain boy, she was sorely disappointed. A few minutes later, the girl spoke, hesitant. "I know you said you're not interested in social media, but…"

"Go on."

"I started following a few female vintage fashion influencers, and…"

"Influencers?"

"Super popular accounts, basically. Other people copy what they do."

"Gotcha. Influence. Makes sense," Claire replied, thinking wryly of how social media had its own language. It was something you had to learn by immersion, like Japanese. She was convinced that wasn't a textbook-only language. "What about them?"

Chapter Eight: Claire

"Some accounts are simple, like I said. A few photos once or twice a week, tags to the stores where they bought the clothes, and how they feel wearing them."

Claire let this process out of respect for her employee. Morgan was convinced that she should do this for some reason. More online exposure would be good for the park, but she knew she would blunder her way through it. She might end up driving people away!

"I'm not sure, honey. You make it sound good, but I already have too much on my plate every day. I don't have time to learn or relearn all of that stuff."

"I could help you." Morgan stopped scrubbing and rested in a squat. "Can I show you the accounts? That way you'd see how easy it is."

"You can show me another day," Claire replied, sighing out the sugary air. "Right now, we've got enough on our hands."

Morgan held her bright red hands up. "For sure! High five?"

"Eh, why not?"

Even with Morgan's prodding, Claire enjoyed spending time with her. She was smart and innovative. Maybe someone like Morgan Sullivan was exactly what the park needed full-time.

She sent her employee home early with a promise not to cut her wage for the day. Then, seeing her own ruined dress, Claire decided she'd better do the same. She texted Kendra with her plans and set off barefoot on the least traveled path possible. It would be best if no one saw...

"What happened to you?"

It would be him. Claire hurried on her way, her nemesis jogging to keep up.

"Oh, nothing, Ryan. Nothing at all."

His guffaw would wake the dead. "I see I'm not the only one who met with a drink disaster."

"Ha-ha. You're hilarious. What do you think this is, comedy hour?"

"Looks it to me." He pulled her to a stop. "Is there anything I can do to help?"

That's when she noticed he'd changed into a fitted t-shirt and shorts. *Oh, mama!*

"No, not at all! We got everything under control. Minor repairs."

"Minor? As in the Mount Vesuvius of slushies?"

"Do you moonlight as a comedian?" she asked, swinging her no-longer-white espadrilles in the air. "If not, you should."

"I'll keep it in mind," he replied with a smirk. His to-die-for hazels roamed over her, half-amused, half-appreciative. "Seriously, can I help?"

"Unless you want to scrub red drink mix out of my hair…" As those eyes met hers, Claire died. *How that must have sounded!* "I've got to go!"

"Suit yourself," he called, letting her cut and run. "You've got my number."

The nerve of that man! But the idea of Ryan's hands anywhere near her hair left her in fits for the rest of the night. What would his fingers feel like running through her loose, wavy tresses? *Whoa, mama, bathe me in ice!*

At home, Claire tossed her dress in the washer with plenty of stain remover. Her shoes went in a baking soda bath. Time would tell the extent of the damage. It was occasions like these she regretted her vintage decisions. Maybe she should wear a park uniform like everyone else.

The bubbles of her shampoo turned pink as she pondered this sobering thought. When she first decided to go the vintage route, even though she found it both freeing and fun, she worried about what other people thought. Most people didn't go around in tailored blouses and heels. Dresses and skirts were typically reserved for special occasions, and modern makeup didn't jive with the 1940s look. It was, in fact, the opposite.

Chapter Eight: Claire

During World War II, a lady's makeup kit consisted of a few essentials and little else. Vanishing cream or foundation, a touch darker than one's skin, a slightly lighter powder, black mascara for both lids, and a bold red lipstick, less common today, were basically it. Some women put Vaseline on their eyebrows, maybe mixed with a bit of burnt cork, but it wasn't required. Eyeshadow, all the rage now, was reserved for evenings and matched the color of one's eyes. In Claire's case, it would've been silvery blue for her blue eyes, but she preferred light brown. She still had silver eyeshadow nightmares from the 2000s.

In her first forays out, she wondered what her friends and neighbors thought. Did they believe she wanted to stand out? Draw attention to herself? That wasn't it at all! Claire simply liked the look better than what was on offer today. It made her feel more feminine and put together. It inspired her, but most of all, it reminded her of her grandmother and how much she'd gone through. Rarely had Claire met a more remarkable woman.

Through the Great Depression and the Second World War, Gran grew up and got married. After the War, she, Grandpa, and the Laniers, their best friends, settled on Pony Island and built the park ride by ride. Thousands of people had partaken of their warmth, love, and hospitality. If Claire could pass on even a spark of her grandmother's dream to guests today, she would consider it a job well done. And the vintage look she adopted as her own helped her do that.

Over time, Claire noticed that people seemed to enjoy seeing what outfits she put together. It brought a smile to the faces of the older generation who remembered their mothers dressing in a similar fashion. Children, especially, loved what they saw as her costume. When she got it right, she did appear like a character from a different era, a time traveler of sorts.

"And now I have pink hair," she deadpanned to the mirror. Uneven splotches all through her wet locks ranged in color from pale pink to the vibrant red of her homemade strawberry jam. Bundled up in her robe, she snapped a sassy photo and sent it to Kendra. Seconds later, she heard a *ding!*

Lugosi: Very nice! You should try blue next.

"Oh, no, no, no!" Claire dropped her phone in the sink trying to figure out how Ryan had gotten the photo. She read the previous message.

Lugosi: I picked up some bleach, and I'm headed over.

"Oh my stars! Oh my stars! Oh…my…stars! Ryan Lanier, you goose!" Instead of texting Kendra, she'd responded to Ryan's unopened message.

Claire: Please tell me you're NOT coming over.

Lugosi: Of course not…unless you need me to.

Her heart fluttered at his last words. Did he mean that as a joke…or was he serious? *Would Ryan drop everything to come to my aid?* As she raided her pantry for cherry drink mix, she wondered – for the first time – if he felt a little something for her too.

Chapter Nine: Ryan

The office was buzzing when Ryan arrived the next morning. He paused by his dad's office, getting a lingering whiff of his favorite aftershave as he picked up a family photo on the desk. "Keep moving forward, Ryan," his dad always said. *"Cherish the past, but don't let it keep you from living in the present."*

It had become Ryan's motto as well, but had he taken it too seriously?

He exchanged a few waves and greetings as he wound his way back to Claire's office. Miss Hattie's words, along with her peach cake, struck a chord. He texted Claire early to ask for another meeting, and he intended to do more listening than talking this time. He wasn't convinced the park could be saved – the numbers screamed 'NO!' – but he would hear Claire out.

It's possible, he admitted to himself, *she saw something I overlooked.*

"How does it look in the back?" he heard her ask someone. Kendra replied.

"Evenly distributed. I think you're good, but girl..."

"I know. I know. I was desperate." He lifted his hand to knock on the cracked door, but Claire's next words stopped him. "I can't believe I sent Ryan that picture! What must he think, that I was flirting with him?"

Ah. That explains that. What did it say that he'd saved said picture? And looked at it...a few times. The unguarded moment was too adorable to delete.

His sister-in-law laughed. "It wasn't like it was inappropriate or anything...was it?"

"No! Do you think I'd take *those* kinds of pictures of myself?" Giggles erupted. He continued to hover, debating what to do. Awkward entry or return later? "At least he was cool about it."

"He's still a great guy, if you'll give him a chance," Kendra said. *Thanks, Sis!* "You know, Travis and I think he..."

Ryan knocked. *Quit while I'm ahead, Kendra!*

"Come in!" Claire called. He peeked his head in, feigning surprise, but she was nowhere in sight.

"Hey!" he said. "Oh, Kendra, you're here too!"

His sister-in-law's gaze narrowed. Had she known he was listening outside?

"Hi, Ryan. We were..."

"Leaving!" Claire blurted from behind a door. "She was leaving. Bye, Kendra. See you later!"

"Bye!" As she passed Ryan, Kendra elbowed him. "Play nice."

"Ouch!"

"Sit down," Claire commanded, invisible. "I'll be out in a sec."

While he waited, Ryan examined her domain. Her desk was scattered with papers, colored folders, highlighters, and felt-tips. Her desk set tickled his memory, and as he examined it further, he realized he'd seen it many times as a small kid. The leather blotter, pen cup, and assorted accessories belonged to her grandmother, the park's former accountant. *Boy, did that lady have a head for numbers.*

"Hey..." Claire said, interrupting his thoughts.

What the..? "Ariel?"

Chapter Nine: Ryan

"Oh, stop it!" she cried, swatting his shoulder on the way to her chair. "I did what I had to do."

"Is it permanent?" he asked, scanning her cherry tresses, softly curled and as luscious as saltwater taffy. *Am I drooling?*

"No. It's drink mix. I figured if I can't beat 'em, I'll join 'em." She twirled one of her pens. "I should apologize about yesterday. Sorry for pouring tea over your head."

"You're fine," he heard himself say, snorting. *Man, if she was a matador, I'd be a bull...even if bulls couldn't see red. That color was oh-so-distracting.*

"Ry-an," Claire sang, "you said you wanted to talk to me?"

"I do, but first, will you sing 'Part of Your World'?"

"Do I look amused?" Then, a smile played on her red, red, red lips. So much red. He glanced down at her dress. Navy blue. Good choice. "Eyes on mine, Ryan."

Now, who was red?

"Should we continue this meeting another time?" she asked, leaning back in her chair. She smoothed her fingers over a curl. "I think my hair has blown your mind."

"Maybe," he replied. "Wanna go for a coke?" On second thought, they didn't need to be anywhere near beverages. "Never mind. You know what, I think I'll find you later."

He left before she could respond. He'd sure bungled that meeting, but how could he help it? Red looked good on her. *Really good.*

During his escape, Ryan ran into Jack – not literally because that would be too much – and for the next couple of hours, the two men worked their way around the park. Not only was the Eye of the Hurricane permanently out of order, but Harvey the seagull, of Seagull Scrambler fame, wasn't going to be repaired any time soon.

"The guys checked it over, and the parts we need cost over a thousand a piece. I think it's time to give Ol' Harvey a burial at sea," Jack said, running a hand over his thick graying hair, "but Claire's determined to fix him. She sure does love this place."

"Don't I know it." Ryan almost launched into his speech about the necessity to sell before his conscience stopped him. He promised himself he would hear Claire out. "How's the Man-of-War?" The Man-of-War was a swing carousel named after the deadly jellyfish.

"Good for now, but after those memes of swings breaking off spammed the internet, it doesn't get as much traffic."

"Hm. I've seen those around. It's a scary concept."

"We perform regular maintenance." Jack scratched his hairline. "Things like that mess with people's heads, and in turn, hurt small businesses like ours. I wish people would watch what they put online."

Ryan squinted toward the 30-foot peak of the Dolphin Dive. "How's the log flume?"

"Running smoothly. So, have you and Claire talked much? I think since I'm retiring at the end of the quarter, she's trying to take care of most things herself. I admire her spunk, but it would be nice if she had someone to lean on."

A squirrel wiggled in Ryan's belly. Jack sure sounded like he was hinting at something.

"A little," he admitted. "We're struggling to see eye to eye."

Jack started walking, motioning for Ryan to follow. "You know, when my wife was alive, there were times we fought like cats and dogs. She could be as stubborn as a barnacle," he winked, "but so was I. This one time, we had a knock-down, drag-out fight over how to load the dish drainer. She won. But I loved that woman so fierce, and she loved me. We always found a way to make it work."

Ryan coughed. "What are you implying? Claire and I are not involved."

"It's simple, son. When two people, romantic or not, choose to work together, even if they fight, they'll always find a way to work things

Chapter Nine: Ryan

out. You and Claire are smart young people who both love this park, am I right?"

"Of course. Pony Island is like a second home, and you know Claire adores it."

"Sounds like you'll eventually come to an agreement."

"Man, I hope you're right."

"I am most of the time," Jack said with another wink, "but don't tell Natalie. I need that woman to keep thinking me humble. How's that for honesty?"

"You sly old dog! I'll keep your secret if you do one thing for me?" Ryan rubbed his hands together, scanning the rose bushes. He plucked the prettiest pink bloom.

"And that is?"

"Give this to Claire, and tell her I'm sorry."

"Shouldn't you do that yourself?"

Ryan saluted as he hiked off. "I've got the dirt on you, remember?"

He could hear Jack's howl as he rounded the bend. It sure was nice to be among old friends.

* * *

"Some decisions need to be made, Ryan," Mr. Dunlap said over the phone. "The PIC is wanting an update."

"We're working on it," he replied, watching some teens strap into the Lighthouse Drop Tower. Even the thought of it made him sick. The lawyer sighed into the receiver.

"Call me as soon as you know something, and Ryan?"

"Yes, sir?"

"Remember that the PIC has requested you ride each of the working rides together. How many have you completed?"

"None." Ryan's stomach flipped over as the drop tower's seats climbed skyward.

"Then, I suggest you find Claire and get that ball rolling."

As luck would have it, the scarlet vision was within shouting distance, chatting with some kids outside of the line for the Lighthouse. He hung back, half-hidden like a spy behind a potted palm. Radiance burst from her like the sunrise over the ocean, lighting the faces of the small group. A tiny girl bounced from foot to foot in front of her, her hands in begging pose. With a nod, Claire grasped her hands and spun the two of them around. The other children joined the circle, and soon, they were dancing around an invisible maypole to music only they could hear.

Ryan watched the scene in slow motion, a part of him wishing he could join in. But he would never be welcome in that inner circle, the realm of kelpies and mermaids visible to dreamers. He was a realist and a grown man. With that sobering thought, he crossed the path into Claire's view. She stopped cold, telling the bad news to the children: *The Big Bad Wolf has arrived. It's time to flee.*

"Hello, Ryan," she said, tucking a vibrant curl behind her ear.

The contrast between Claire-before-Ryan and Claire-after-Ryan stabbed the wolf in the heart. He'd hurt her, he knew, but he was trying to make things better. Instead of remorse, a flicker of irritation flamed up. *Why won't she work with me? Why am I always the one to make things right?* Shoving aside his confusing feelings, he widened his stance. He wasn't going to let Little Red Riding Hood push him around.

"Hello, Red. Dunlap called for a progress report, but as we haven't made any, I had to put him off."

Claire glared at him and pointed to the drop tower. "Didn't he say we have to ride every ride? C'mon, before it breaks down."

She did not *say that!*

Claire claimed two seats on the next ride. Inside, Ryan wanted to bolt for the hills of Tennessee, but looking like a weakling in front of

Chapter Nine: Ryan

Claire and the dozen guests wasn't an option. Her baby blues sparked with challenge. *She knows.*

"I can't wait," Ryan said through clenched teeth as he clamped himself in. *I'm going to be sick!*

He jumped when she patted his hand. "Poor baby! Do you want to get off?"

"No."

The ride started, and his feet left the safety of terra firma. Spectators shrunk, and the air thinned.

I can't breathe!

"Don't die on me now, Ryan Lanier," Claire called. "You got this."

Chapter Ten: Ryan

I got this. I got this. They reached the top, a mere one hundred feet over the park with a reportedly stunning view of the ocean or mainland, depending on which side you were on – not that Ryan would know – and dropped. *I don't got this!*

Back up, then down. Up, up, up…down…down. Up. Down. Down. And down. As the ride came to a stop, he peeled his hands off the handles and jerked free of the harness. The nearby bushes would have to do.

She made apologies to their guests as he retched into the shrubbery. A moment later, he felt a hand on his shoulder. A tissue appeared next to his face.

"Can I get you anything?" Claire asked, rubbing circles on his back.

"Water would be nice," he replied. She helped him stagger to a bench before heading off to the nearest drink cart. Upon her return, she twisted off the cap and shoved the bottle in his face.

"Drink this."

Shaky, he spilled water down his shirt. Her hands wrapped around his for an assist. After a few swigs, he leaned back, feeling like the world's biggest wuss.

Chapter Ten: Ryan

"I hate that ride."

"I know, but hey, you're alive, aren't you?"

"No thanks to you."

He sipped some more while Claire propped her elbow on the back of the bench, her body facing him.

"Jack brought your peace offering."

"It must have been a dud," he replied. "You tried to kill me."

"I can't decide whether to be mad at you for snapping off one of my grandmother's prized roses…or to forgive you."

"The latter?"

"You made fun of me."

Loopy, he reached for a strand of her hair and wrapped it loosely around his finger. "I've decided this red suits you."

"Yeah?"

"Yeah. Claire Hensley, you're a firecracker."

Had this been a cheesy romance movie – and had his mouth not tasted like vomit – they might have shared a moment. Gazes locked, glances to lips, heads tilting. But did any of that happen? *No. It didn't.*

"Claire! Claire!" yelled a crew member running up. "Reynaldo's at it again."

"Women's restroom?" she replied, tearing away from Ryan.

"No. The men's."

"Oh no."

Ryan pushed to his feet. "Can I help?"

Claire scanned him up and down. "How are you with peacocks? Never mind. Come on!"

* * *

"Oh good! You're here," a pale-faced custodian said. The young woman was green about the gills. "He's in the men's restroom…and the carnage.

Claire, I can't..."

"It's okay," Claire replied, exhibiting some deep breathing exercises. Their employee followed suit. "In and out. In and out. Now, tell me what happened."

The young woman looked over at Ryan, uncertain, and he smiled encouragingly. He was dying to know what she meant by carnage...*no pun intended.*

"I saw the whole thing," she began, wringing her hands. "Reynaldo was going crazy, chasing something through the bushes. He burst out on the tail of a huge snake! When it slithered into the restroom, Reynaldo pounced. He grasped it by the neck and started shaking and shaking and..."

Ryan caught Claire before she hit the pavement. He'd forgotten her fear of snakes. Pulling her into his arms – to steady her, of course – he cut the young woman off.

"We've got the picture."

"I think he's going to eat it."

"I didn't know peacocks ate snakes," a crew bystander said.

"Venomous ones too," replied another. "I heard that Rajas in India used to keep them to guard their palaces from cobras. They'll even attack king cobras!"

A collective 'ooh' hummed through the growing crowd. Claire remained in his sturdy embrace, resting her pale face against his shoulder, her eyes closed and her breathing shallow.

"Claire?" he whispered, ignoring the curious stares of their employees. Most of them probably didn't know who he was. "Do you need to sit down?"

Her arms wound around his waist as she burrowed her face into his chest with a shudder. "No, but I don't...do...snakes."

Ryan hated to feel less than platonic about this moment. He really did. But the thrill of having Claire in his arms for the first time – no

Chapter Ten: Ryan

matter the reason – overrode all sensors.

However, there was still the matter of the snake-chasing peacock. When no one else took the initiative, Ryan made up his mind. He'd killed a few snakes in his day, for safety, not for sport. He'd have a talk with Reynaldo, man to man, and get him to vacate the facilities.

"Can you stand on your own?" he asked. "I'm not afraid of snakes. I'll go in."

Claire eased away, leaving a void behind. The skin of her face was translucent.

"Be careful, Ryan. Reynaldo is more stubborn than you." Her little smile made his heart skip a beat. He puffed his chest, preening like a…peacock. *Hm.*

"I got this, Claire. No worries."

A hush fell over the crowd as he strode forward, false bravado masking his inner turmoil. The peacocks were a recent addition to the park, within the past five years. He knew next to nothing about handling them, or any other fowl for that matter.

Compared to the bright daylight, the interior of the men's room was like a cave. He paused in the short hall to let his vision adjust and to listen for the victor. He had no idea who would win Snake vs. Peacock. *What if Reynaldo met his match?*

Quiet squawks and grunts filtered to his ears as he tiptoed to the corner. The peacock stood tail down in front of the sinks, a dead garter snake at his feet. The meal was in progress.

"It's an Eastern Garter Snake," he called. "And it's dead."

"I don't care what kind of snake it is!" Claire replied. "The only good snake is a dead snake."

"Snakes are essential to the balance of nature. They keep the rodent population under control."

"Ryan! Get Reynaldo out of there. He didn't trap anyone, did he?"

Looking around, Ryan didn't see any guests. He called out to make sure.

"The place is empty, except for…"

"Ryan!"

He moved nearer, palms out. "Hey there, big guy."

Reynaldo's sharp beak gleamed under the fluorescents.

"Look at you, snake killer, tough man."

His long tail feathers began to quiver. Ryan crept sideways. Maybe he could herd him out.

"I'm impressed." The peacock stepped in front of his prey. "Don't worry. It's all yours. How about you grab it and run?"

Chirp-squawk!

"Oh, I see. You don't like that plan."

"Ryan? Are you still alive?" Claire called. "Do I need to text Travis?"

"No. Rey and I are having a heart-to-heart. Right, man?"

Reynaldo screeched in denial.

"I'm texting Travis!"

"C'mon, dude," Ryan said, easing closer. "There are more snakes outside, bigger ones, tastier ones."

Shaking his head, the bird lifted his tail, the dozens of eyes flashing in the artificial light. Things were getting serious. Measuring the space between the bird and the stalls, Ryan calculated his next move, factoring in the water…and stuff…on the 1960s sea green tile floor. *What if I slip?*

"Negativity breeds fear," he chanted to himself. "You got this."

Soaring, Ryan was off. His trusty sneakers kept him upright as he skidded past Reynaldo to the far end of the room. The peacock turned in a blind rage and attacked!

At least that was the story he would stick to. In reality, he slipped on peacock excrement and went down, sliding past the bird, the dead garter, and the six stalls. When he came to a stop, his hip was on fire and his wrist throbbed. The good news was that Reynaldo, who'd had

Chapter Ten: Ryan

enough of the crazy human, grabbed his snack and hightailed it out of there. As a cheer erupted from outside, Ryan lay on the cool, wet tiles, dying a little inside.

"Ryan!" Travis cried upon entering. Claire, on his heels, gasped.

"Is he dead?"

"I don't think so," Ryan replied, easing up on his uninjured side. Claire dropped to her knees, frantically touching his forehead, cheeks, shoulders, arms...

"What happened?"

"I slipped." When he tried to stand, he collapsed in a heap. "Ack!"

"Man down!" Travis said, draping Ryan's good arm over his shoulders. Claire helped them rise, hovering like a mother peahen all the way out the door.

In the First Aid Center, the nurse, a former paramedic, examined his injuries while Claire and Travis waited on the other side of the curtain.

"Well, Ryan, it looks like your hip is bruised pretty good, but if any complications arise, go see a doctor." She gently flexed his wrist and fingers. He gasped at the pain. "I think it's a sprain, but I'd like you to go for an x-ray to make sure. Do you have someone to take you?"

Having endured similar football injuries in high school, Ryan resigned himself. "Travis?"

"Sorry, Bro," he replied. "Kendra and I have this thing tonight."

"O-kay..."

"I can take you," Claire interjected. "It's my fault, after all."

"How is it your..." Ryan paused, snapping with his good hand. "Oh, the snake."

As they exited, Claire offered her shoulders as a crutch. As Ryan nestled her under his arm, being sure not to lean too hard, his pre-Reynaldo feelings came rushing back. *I could get used to this.*

Chapter Eleven: Claire

"The Man-of-War is down," squawked the operator over the walkie-talkie app. Claire buried her face in her hands, pushing the heels into her eyes. *Just what we need.*

Leaving her office, she hurried toward the swing carousel, plastering on the fakest of fake smiles. The fiasco with Reynaldo the previous day, not to mention Ryan's injuries, ate at her. She never should have let him go in there, co-owner or not. It would've been better to have called wildlife control, but the snake shut her down completely.

Ryan probably thought she had a vendetta against him. First, she forced him on the ride she knew he hated, after which, he threw up. Add to that a sprained wrist – confirmed by an x-ray – a bruised hip, and a crusty layer of peacock poo and…stuff. She wouldn't blame him if he hightailed it back to Nashville and never spoke to her again.

That's what she would have wanted a couple days ago, but now…the memory of being in his arms, the feeling of safety and strength, both would be hard to forget. But that was exactly what she must do. He was gung ho on selling, and he could easily use the Reynaldo incident as leverage. She could see the headline: "Man Attacked by Crazy Snake-Eating Bird at Local Amusement Park – Details, Page 4."

Chapter Eleven: Claire

"What seems to be the problem?" she asked the operator upon arrival at the Man-of-War. Guests were being evacuated one by one using a scissor lift. The crew member at the exit attempted to placate them with snack coupons. *Was anyone paying for food anymore?*

"The tilt mechanism appears to be stuck," he replied. "It's a wonder no one was hurt when I brought the ride to a stop."

Claire pushed her fingers into her hair. "This is a disaster! Let's hope we don't get sued."

"Can they sue us if they aren't injured?"

"I'm sure they could find a way," she replied. "Plaintiffs win cases based on much less nowadays."

As maintenance checked the ride over, Claire called her mom. Natalie answered on the second ring.

"This is a surprise. I hope nothing is wrong."

"The Man-of-War is down," Claire said, pushing through the ride's exit gate. "That's three rides out of order with little chance of reopening this season. What am I going to do?"

"I'm sorry, baby." Restaurant noises clattered in the background before giving way to windy static. Her mom must have stepped outside. "What does Ryan say about it?"

"I haven't told him yet. Where are you?"

"I met Helene for brunch. We're going to the art gallery and may do some shopping."

"Oh! Sorry to bother you, Mom."

"You're never a bother," Natalie replied, her familiar reminder a balm to Claire's soul. If there was one person she could count on, it was her mother. "You know you can call me any time, night or day."

"I know." Claire passed the park's old-time photo studio, now closed, and her heart gave a pang. The Old West had been her dad's passion, and it was his idea to insert a piece of it into coastal South Carolina. "Hey, remember those photos Dad made us pose for when I was twelve?

He made you and me wear those corseted dresses and humongous feathered hats, but he strolled out of the dressing room dressed as a pirate?"

Natalie laughed until she snorted. "Your father was a nut, that's for sure. He always kept me entertained."

"I miss him, Mom."

"I do too, Claire. Every day."

"How's Helene?"

"It hit her pretty hard last night, but she insisted upon getting out."

Claire sensed a pregnant pause. "What is it, Mom?"

"I don't mean to pry, but…"

"Mom…"

"I know you and Ryan don't see eye to eye on the park's future, but don't forget he recently lost his father. He's not one to express his feelings, but Helene says he hasn't been sleeping well, on top of his injuries."

Claire blew out her breath. While she hadn't forgotten Mr. Lanier's passing, in all the turmoil, Ryan's grief was not forefront in her mind.

"You're right, and I should tell him about the Man-of-War as soon as possible. He needs to know."

After signing off, Claire shot Ryan a text. Another text pinged in immediately, but this one was from Jack asking her to come to his office at her earliest convenience. Now was as good a time as any.

"One moment, Claire," Jack said, covering the receiver of his office telephone. "It's my daughter."

As they finished up their conversation, Claire examined the pictures on her boss's walls. One of him and her mom grinning like two teenagers in front of the island's seasonal ice cream stand made her smile, despite the pang. *Mom's moving on.*

"Thank you for coming," he said, rising. "She was updating me on Wish Granted's most recent opportunities."

Chapter Eleven: Claire

Wish Granted was a non-profit serving terminally ill children in South Carolina. Each month, they granted one wish with the help of donors and local businesses. During its brief five-year run, the organization amassed the support of the state's wealthiest residents. Organizations considered it an honor to be chosen as host.

"She's on the board now, right?"

"Hm? Oh, yes." Jack strayed to the same photo, and he ran a shaky hand through his hair. "I didn't expect this to be so hard."

"What?" she asked, shifting on her wedges. "Spit it out, Jack!"

"I want to marry your mom." Although Claire suspected as much, the words caught her off guard. Jack's face fell. "You don't want me to."

"No! I mean, not at all." *That's not what I meant!*

"Oh. I'm glad I asked, then. I didn't want to ask her without your blessing."

Claire grabbed his arm. "You have it! Oh, Jack, I sure made a pickle of that."

"Then, you're happy with me asking your mom to marry her?"

"Yes! You're practically family already."

"Thank you. You too, kid."

She nudged him with her elbow. "Do you need my help with anything?"

"No," he replied with a wink, "I've got it covered."

As Claire left Jack's office, even though she was happy for them, she couldn't help but feel a sting of longing for her own relationship. *It must be amazing to know someone wanted to spend the rest of their life with you.*

Back in her office, Claire found a text from Ryan waiting. He merely asked about the cost of repairs, keeping his opinion to himself. Once that was sent, she pulled a spreadsheet up on her computer and tried to get to work, but her thoughts bounced around like a kangaroo on espresso.

It would be nice to have someone to share these burdens with, someone who was on the same page. Someone to go home to.

I should get a dog.

"But not until we get the park back on stable ground. I don't have time for love and romance…or a pet. Maybe I never will."

But she didn't see any way out of this mess. Ryan's push to sell was taking its toll on her nerves, not only because it annoyed her, but also, she feared he was right. The park was off track, and the bills were mounting up. If they were down to a miracle, they were out of luck.

And then there was the looming question: *Why was Ryan pushing for a quick sale?*

He was eager to get back to Nashville. She'd pushed off this line of thought due to the lack of evidence, but now, she couldn't unthink it. Was someone waiting for him? A…*gulp*…girlfriend?

The green monster of jealousy reared its ugly head before she smothered it. No one had mentioned a girlfriend. But why would they? It wasn't as if she and Ryan were friends. And there was always the possibility he was keeping a relationship secret from his family.

Why am I jealous? I don't want Ryan Lanier anymore! That ship sailed the moment he left without saying goodbye.

"Ugh!" Claire leapt from her chair. She needed a distraction which the spreadsheet was clearly not providing. Spying Kendra out a window, she sought out her friend.

Kendra was on her cell, her back to Claire's approach. "Yes, that would be a good time."

When Claire's shoe crunched on a stray stick, her bestie whirled around. She held the device to her chest before mumbling a quick, "I've got to go."

"I didn't mean to interrupt," Claire said, hesitating. "I should let you finish your call."

"No," Kendra replied, not moving. "What's up?"

Chapter Eleven: Claire

Claire flapped her hand. "I'm worried about the park." *And you. I'm worried about you.* What was going on with her friend?

"I know. How are things with Ryan? Is he coming around?"

"Not as far as I can tell," Claire replied with a snort. "He's convinced he's right."

"As are you."

"Hey, whose side are you on?"

Kendra's laugh was shallow, but before she could respond, another call came in. *Sorry,* she mouthed, scooting off. Claire's worry amplified tenfold. Why wouldn't Kendra confide in her?

Chapter Twelve: Claire

On her lunch break, Claire made a round of the park's gift shops and merchandise stands. Her first stop was the main shop at the front of the park. It carried an assortment of t-shirts, tote bags, and toys, as well as some essentials guests tended to forget.

In the past, the shelves and racks brimmed full of souvenirs, but as the park's fortunes declined, so did the choices on offer. They had to make some tough decisions regarding what to keep, what to discontinue, and what to downgrade on quality. Sales were down, but as they received few complaints, it wasn't worth the worry.

After a look-over, needlessly straightening things as she passed, Claire made her way to the register. The long-time cashier smiled wearily.

"How are things today, Jean?" Claire asked, giving her friend a side hug.

"Slow as usual, darlin'. A few sales, but most folks just look." She lowered her voice. "I overheard one lady saying that the t-shirt material was too cheap for the price. I'm sorry, Claire, but I have to agree."

"I know. I don't disagree, but the better-quality shirts come with a

Chapter Twelve: Claire

higher price tag, and no one was buying those."

"The big item today is sunscreen. I pushed the magnets and snow globes, but no one is biting." Jean leaned over, pursing her fuchsia lips. "I tried to convince them the snow globe gives the illusion of cool weather. They didn't believe me."

"At least you tried," Claire replied, laughing. "Can I do anything for you while I'm here?"

"No, dear, but thank you. I'm hardly run off my feet, and the movement does me good."

The story was the same at the stands she passed. A few sales here and there but nothing big. One other shop remained open. The small specialty stores, which boomed with sales until the late 1990s, were all locked up.

Claire's favorite store had always been the Christmas shop. Ryan's grandfather, a fighter pilot in the War, was a master woodcarver. In his spare time, he'd carved thousands of small animals and sea-themed objects out of driftwood. They were sold as ornaments, along with glass globes, resin figurines, and scavenged shells. Claire cherished her own small collection. She wondered if Ryan kept any for his Nashville Christmas tree.

Did the Grinch even put up a Christmas tree?

The second open shop was located next to the secondary station for the Pony Island Express Train, one of the park's oldest rides. The intern manning the counter, upon seeing Claire, shoved his cell in his pocket and stood at attention.

"At ease, soldier," Claire teased. "I can see it's slow."

"I'm sorry, Miss Claire. I wasn't texting. I was checking some game stats."

"What sport?"

The teen's ears turned crimson. "They're for a video game my friends and I play. There's a tournament on."

"Oh, I see. How are things in the shop today?"

His flush deepened. "You're the first person I've seen all day."

"No wonder you're bored." She inspected the space and found it impeccable. "It looks great in here. I guess if you want something to do, you can...I'm sorry. I can't think of anything."

"I'll stay off my phone. I know it's against policy."

"Thanks, Noah. Enjoy your lunch."

As she headed back to the office for her own chicken salad, she sent a text to Kendra to ask her to shuffle the merchandise schedule a bit. It was probably time to close another shop.

* * *

"Hey! Shouldn't you be resting?" Claire called. Ryan whirled around with a grimace.

"I was going stir-crazy, so I decided to take a walk and ended up here." They met in front of the Loggerheads Bumper Cars. Each car was painted to look like a sea turtle. Ryan took one more step closer. "I can't stay away."

The deep timbre of his voice said one thing while his relaxed stance claimed another. Ignoring the urge to probe, Claire broke eye contact.

"How are you feeling?"

"Less sore. I'm ready to get this splint off." He motioned toward the bumper cars. "Shall we?"

"Can you drive?"

"One-handed? No problem."

As they entered the queue, she leaned back against the metal partition. "You can get me back. Rough me up a bit."

"Don't tempt me," he replied, mimicking her stance. "That Red 40 must be strong stuff. Your hair hasn't faded."

"I wouldn't know." Claire felt her face heat. Would he think she was

Chapter Twelve: Claire

gross? "I wash my hair once or twice a week."

Ryan's complexion darkened. "I reckon," his voice squeaked, "that would slow the fading."

They moved forward. Claire distracted herself by calculating how many ride groups were in line. They should be in the next one.

"While we're sharing, I wash mine every other day," he stated. "Soothing organic oatmeal-lavender almond milk shampoo. I use it on my beard too. It's a lifesaver."

"Are you serious?" Claire felt a giggle bubbling up. "You use organic shampoo?"

As space appeared in front of them, he touched the small of her back. "Wouldn't you like to know?"

With him behind her now, she couldn't see his face, but she feared hers was as red as her hair. As the seconds passed like minutes, his hand lingered on the waistband of her skirt. The wind blew her hair back, exposing her to Ryan's secret scrutiny…or dare she wish, admiration. His exhale dusted her ear and neck.

"We're up."

When she sucked in a breath, she caught a bubble and started coughing. Tears streamed down her cheeks. She stumbled to the nearest loggerhead as Ryan selected a nearby car, his brows knit together with concern.

"Do you need some water?" he asked when she was finally able to take a deep inhale.

"No." *Cough, cough.* "I'm…fine." The dratted tickle finally quit.

"If you're sure."

"Yep." The countdown began. *3-2-1!* "Let's do this!"

Energy hummed from the floor to Claire's turtle car. Stomping on the gas, she revved out of Ryan's way, swinging back for a hit. Laughter and cheers echoed all over the floor for the two-minute ride. Ryan came back hard before being pummeled by a preteen boy. Claire went to his rescue as the music stopped. He helped her out and walked her to the exit. Outside, she motioned to his wrist.

"How are you feeling?"

"Right as rain."

"Does anyone say that anymore?" she asked, the vintage expression warming her heart.

"I just did." When he bumped into her, she resisted the urge to hook his arm, gripping her hands in front of her. He had no such touching restriction, steering her by the shoulders.

"Where are we going in such a hurry?"

"The restroom."

"The restroom? Ryan, if you need to go, you don't have to wait for me."

"I don't need to go."

"Then why…"

"Look in the mirror."

The mirror? Knowing flooded her, and she ran in. One glance confirmed her fears.

"Guess I should've gone with waterproof mascara," she said, grabbing a handful of paper towels, "even though it isn't historically accurate!"

Chapter Thirteen: Ryan

When Claire emerged from the restroom sans runny mascara, Ryan caught a flash of the makeup-free girl he once knew. His heart did the Carolina shag, urging him forward, while caution held him back. That girl was gone, replaced by a beautiful but fierce woman. Claire was a bit like a sleeping tiger: pretty to look at but terrifying to rouse.

"That doesn't happen often," she said, shyly tucking her hair behind her ear. "Why didn't you tell me before we got on the ride?"

"And spoil your war paint? Never!" Taking a chance, he soft-slugged her arm. "I'd say you've earned a treat. I'm buying."

"You're an owner, Ryan," she replied. "We don't have to pay." The intimacy of 'we' rubbed over him like smooth velvet.

"I'm going to anyway. We need the money. So, what will it be?"

When Claire batted her light brown lashes, he wondered what she was up to. "Anything?"

"A treat, Claire. As in singular. But yes, anything."

She laid her hand on his chest, burning through to his soul. As she grasped the material, tugging him forward, a single thought assailed him.

She wants me!

His arms flew out, prepared to bring Claire in for a long-awaited kiss...and grasped air. He stumbled after her, leashed by her grip on his shirtfront.

"I know what I want more than anything!" she said over her shoulder. She released him with a magnificent smile, full of love and desire. *Me! Me! Please pick me!* "Funnel cake with powdered sugar, chocolate and vanilla swirl soft serve, strawberries, and whipped cream!"

"Heh," he replied, jogging to keep up. That was a tough combo to beat. "I was thinking the same thing."

* * *

Whoever said fried dough can't heal broken hearts – that's nobody, in case you were wondering – never tasted a Pony Island funnel cake. Ryan devoured his – Claire wasn't about to share her $15 delicacy – hoping the pending sugar coma would bring his priorities into focus.

One, he had limited vacation days left to sort out the future of the amusement park before he had to return to work. Two, Dominic was counting on him to help prepare for Michael's March. Three, Claire wasn't and never had been interested in him. Why was he letting his crushes give him hope? And that was crushes *plural*. He'd never gotten over his first crush on the girl Claire, and now, he was falling for the woman Claire hook, line, and sinker.

The answer was to keep his distance, but that was hard to do when they were required to ride the rides together and work out a solution. His attempt at negotiating was taken as railroading, but selling still seemed to him the best option.

"You're lost in thought," Claire said, licking her fingers. "Thinking about your dad? It's hard to lose a parent. When I lost my dad, it was like half my world was gone."

Chapter Thirteen: Ryan

"I miss him," he replied, pushing his plate away, "but after the first heart attack, I guess I started the grief process. His death was hard at first, but now, I just want to move on. It's what he would want too."

"Sorry."

"Don't be. I guess I'm not the sentimental type. Is that terrible?"

"No, Ryan. Everyone grieves in their own way."

She took one quiet, final lick. Ryan forced himself to look away. He didn't want to see her bliss morph into blind rage.

"We're down to nine rides," he replied, wadding up his napkin. "At what point do you think potential guests will reach their limit?"

Instead of the outburst he expected, Claire turned thoughtful. "I'm not sure, but I believe we can make this work. I'm not ready to give up."

"I'm not suggesting we give up, but…"

"Spit it out, Ryan."

"The price the park will fetch is directly correlated to its condition. If we wait too long, the selling price might not cover our debts or provide enough to compensate our employees, not to mention give you, Travis, and Kendra something to live on in the meantime." He risked a glance and found her focus glued to her empty paper plate. "It's not about the money, Claire. I care about my family. I care about…you."

"I appreciate your concern, but my welfare is not my top priority. This place," she made a sweeping gesture, "is more than an income for most of us. It's home. You don't give up your home when things get tough. You figure out a way to make it work. 'Make do and mend,' you know?"

Memories assailed him of their grandmothers saving margarine tubs and patching up clothes. There was nothing more disappointing to a young boy than opening a tub of Cool Whip to find sliced onions.

"Claire, this isn't the same. People are counting on us. If we wait too late to decide, and the park tanks, they'll be out of a job with no assistance while they hunt for another. Is that what you want?"

They rose in unison, and he grabbed their things to throw away. Claire walked next to him, her skirt swishing against his shorts.

"You know it's not," she said, placing her hand into the crook of his elbow. The unexpected touch sent his senses reeling, but the sadness in her voice burned. "But Ryan, do you have no hope?"

One more second, and he might promise her the moon. He gave her hand a gentle squeeze before pulling away.

"I can't say that I do, but we don't have to decide right now."

"Guess that's better than nothing."

* * *

"Hey, Mom," Ryan said upon entering her house. Helene was sitting at the kitchen table doing finances.

"Hi, sweetie." Pulling off her glasses, she rubbed her eyes with the back of her hand. "I'm trying to keep my mind busy."

Ryan pulled two bottles of water from the refrigerator. "Want one?"

"Sure." She motioned to her laptop. "I'm glad I stayed on top of our household accounts. It would have been a nightmare to have all this thrust upon me after your father's…"

"Is everything all right?"

"It seems to be." Helene laid her hand on his splint. "How are you feeling?"

"Ready to get this thing off," he replied with a wry laugh. "It itches!"

"I know what you mean." She returned to her work, but knowing his mom, it was a ruse. "Where've you been? Seeing Claire?"

He feigned shock. "As a matter of fact, I was with Claire until a few minutes ago. How did you know?"

"A mom never reveals her sources." When he didn't elaborate, she waved her pen at him. "Bring me up to speed. Where are we with the

Chapter Thirteen: Ryan

park?"

"A stalemate." His mom frowned. "I wish we knew who the PIC is. Why won't they come forward? This would be easier with a third party...but at least, we're not fighting now. That's good."

She pointed to a bit of powdered sugar on his shirt. "You sure about that?"

"Ha-ha. That was me. We went for a snack after riding the Loggerheads."

"Ooo, like a date?" Helene sparkled like a cartoon dog spotting a bone.

"No, definitely not a date. She had a makeup mishap, and I wanted our strictly professional meeting to end on a high note."

"A makeup mishap?" Her eyebrows hit the roof as she searched his face, neck, and collar. "Please tell me we're talking lipstick."

"Mom, sheesh! No. She started coughing, and the tears made her mascara run."

"Drat. I was hoping she finally admitted it." She appeared to check some figures as he stared at her.

"Admitted what?"

The front door opened, and Travis stormed in, retrieving a soda from the fridge. Helene clammed up as Ryan's heart pounded in his ears. She knew about his crush, but did she know something about Claire's feelings too? He had to be reading too much into it.

"What's wrong, honey?" she asked his brother.

"Nothing."

"Try that again, Bro," Ryan replied. "You're guzzling a Coke and steaming."

Travis thumped the half-drained can on the counter. "I'm fine. Kendra's fine. It's nothing like that."

"Then, what?" their mom asked.

"We're frustrated, is all. Sorry. I stopped by to check on y'all, but I

77

can't stay."

"I'm fine," Helene replied, deferring to Ryan.

"I'm good."

Crushing the can, Travis tossed it in the recycling bin. "Let me know if you need anything. See y'all later."

"That was weird," Ryan said to his mom. He turned to find her thoughtful.

"He's been like that for a few months. Kendra too. I can't figure it out, but I don't want to pry." She rolled the arm of her reading glasses between her thumb and forefinger. "Their marriage seems solid, so I assume they'll tell me when I need to know."

"Think she's pregnant?"

Helene frowned. "I don't think so. I don't know, of course, but this feels different."

As he laid his head on his pillow that night, Ryan realized he hadn't prodded his mom about what she hoped Claire finally admitted. Maybe tomorrow.

Chapter Fourteen: Ryan

Helene was gone by the time Ryan went down for breakfast. In the light of day, his mom's speculation about Claire seemed a less concrete route to follow. It might give him false hope… or confirm his fears. Neither would give him confidence around Claire.

After he buried his conflicting feelings in a microwave breakfast sandwich, he headed to the park. Claire was AWOL from the office. Instead of texting her, he opted for a stroll.

Mornings on Pony Island were the complete opposite of Nashville. Instead of the hustle and bustle of the city, people and cars zooming in a million different directions, Island Time moved at a slower pace. Even the sun lingered in its ocean bed.

Finding a place on the railing, Ryan stared out to sea. Sailboats bobbed on the horizon, jet skis shot out water flumes like horses' tails, and paragliders floated on the gentle winds. In the park, guests strolled from ride to ride, stopping at food kiosks or browsing for souvenirs. Everyone appeared to be enjoying themselves, but numbers were thin. He didn't spot any purchase lines, only those for the rides.

While he wished with all his heart for the park to succeed, they couldn't force people to spend money. And if they upped the prices too

Do I Look Amused?

much to compensate, they might lose their loyal customers. Hitting people in the wallet never endeared them to you.

Screams erupted from the left. Before he could move, Ryan went down with a mass of faux fur and shiny scales. A very real person – male, by the sound of it – groaned from within the Sea-Horse suit.

"Are you okay?" Ryan asked, scrambling up. Twin girls with purple shirts displaying golden '7's followed with trembling lower lips.

"Did we kill her?" one asked, tears on the horizon.

"Ouch," the male voice said, the Sea-Horse's massive head lifting as its hooves pushed it to sitting. The girls' gap-toothed mouths dropped open. Ryan attempted a redirect.

"Have you been on the Whirlpool?" He pointed toward the Tilt-A-Whirl. "It's over yonder."

"Can we go, Mom?"

"Please, Dad?"

"Good idea," their mother said, hustling them away. The father lingered, shaking his head.

"I'm so sorry, man," he said to the mascot. "Twins, they get crazy sometimes."

"We're cool," the Sea-Horse replied, letting the men pull him to his feet. "I've experienced worse, like the time that kid threw up…"

"O-kay," Ryan interrupted, hushing the mascot with a hand on its front leg. "We're sorry, sir, for any trauma your daughters might have…"

"No, I'm sorry. Like I said, they're," he waved jazz hands, "nuts sometimes. Y'all take care!"

After the dad jogged off to his family, Ryan ushered the Sea Horse to the crew area. The removal of the head revealed a teenaged boy with shaggy brown hair.

"Are you sure you're all right?" Ryan asked. "I'm sorry. I don't know your name."

Chapter Fourteen: Ryan

"Yeah. Just bruises," the boy said. "Name's Jacob. You're Travis's brother, right?"

"That's me – Ryan. Here, let me help you get that suit off."

As they dissected the Sea Horse, Jacob monologued. Ryan tried to keep up, but the kid's slang left him marooned. *Man, I feel old.* Suddenly, Jacob, his bottom half still in the suit, went silent. Ryan found him drooling over a pretty teen girl with long ginger hair. As she passed, she gave a little wave.

"Hey, Jacob. And you're Ryan Lanier, right?"

"I am."

"This...this...is...Morgan," Jacob stuttered. "She works here too."

Morgan touched her nametag as she looked down at her uniform. Ryan held back a chuckle.

"It's nice to meet you, Morgan."

"You too, sir." She bit her lip as she took in Jacob's costume situation and backed up a step. "I'm on break. It was nice to meet you, Mr. Lanier. Bye, Jacob."

Once she was out of earshot, and Jacob was out of the mermaid tail, he deflated on the bench of a picnic table.

"She's gorgeous, and I'm a dork."

Ryan's heart went out to the kid. He had no idea of Morgan's feelings – teen girls were impossible to read – but he knew a heartsick teenaged boy when he saw one. Sitting next to him, Ryan propped his ankle on his knee, trying to look like a cool adult. Jacob gave him the side-eye.

"Have you asked her out?"

"Are you crazy? She'd never be interested in me." He pointed to the limp kelpie. "What girl wants to date a guy who dresses up as a female mer-horse? Dude, I wear a bikini. That is so not cool."

"When you put it like that...you could always ask to transfer to something cooler."

Jacob shook his head. "Miss Claire gave me a chance when no one else on the island would hire me. I won't let her down."

Ryan clamped a hand on his shoulder. "You're a good man, Jacob. With commitment like that, you'll get the girl." He waggled his eyebrows. "Women can't resist a man who can commit."

"Really?"

"Sure. You need help getting that suit back to wardrobe? It needs a good cleaning."

Jacob thumped his head on the table. "Shoot! The costume lady's going to kill me."

"C'mon. I'm a witness to the mauling. I'll help you sort things out."

"Thanks, sir. You're a lifesaver."

"Don't mention it."

* * *

"Jacob said you saved his hide with wardrobe," Claire said when they met up later. "Thank you."

It was nearing lunchtime, and the restaurant and food kiosks were picking up steam. Maybe they would break even today. Bolstering his happy mood, Ryan felt her praise to the tips of his toes.

"No problem. He reminds me of myself at that age."

"What? You were one of the cool kids," she slugged his arm, "football player and all."

"I wasn't a 'cool' football player."

"I thought all football players were 'cool,'" she replied, forming air quotes. Memories of being bullied in the locker room for being a numbers nerd haunted him.

"No, not all." Had the stories not filtered to the rest of the school? "Wanna get lunch?"

She caught the change of subject and grabbed his arm. "Is it something I said?"

Chapter Fourteen: Ryan

"No, but not all of my high school memories are worth remembering." Claire's hand slid up to his shoulder, and he resisted the urge to touch her bare tricep. "I'm sorry. I didn't know. You always seemed like you had it together."

"Guess I had you fooled." When she pulled away, summer turned to winter. "With the lunch rush, now might be a good time for a ride. How about the Rolling Waves?"

"The roller coaster?" she repeated with a gulp. "Now?"

"What is this?" he asked, remembering. "That's your 'drop-tower,' isn't it? I can't believe I forgot."

"Not exactly, but it's not my favorite."

He sidled up to her. "When was the last time you rode it?"

"Honestly, not but a few times since high school. It's fun, but I get so nervous!" She wrung her hands as she stared at the wooden coaster. He wrapped his hands around hers, gently tugging. The innocent touch tingled like an electric shock.

"I'll be right there with you," he whispered, his breath stirring her slightly faded red hair, "Ariel."

When she rolled her eyes, he almost regretted the nickname, but it kept him from making a fool of himself. If only the proverbial crab would get the message. Ryan could not kiss the girl!

"Let's get it over with."

Chapter Fifteen: Claire

"I'll be right there with you, Ariel."

Even though they parted ways an hour ago, the thrill of the coaster mixed with spending another fun time with Ryan buzzed in Claire's veins. She hadn't realized it, but she'd been stuck in her comfort zone for years. She loved how he encouraged her to live boldly.

Loved. When she was a teen, she doodled hearts with their names and initials. Claire & Ryan. Ryan & Claire. R & C 4 Ever. Mr. and Mrs. Ryan Lanier. Her young heart fancied herself in love, but she hardly knew what real love was. Even now, after a decade of being an 'adult,' Claire wondered if she would ever find it and what it would be like if she did.

The feel of Ryan lingered on her fingers and palms, making her itch to touch him again. Other than a few random touches, their teen selves made little physical contact. What was it about being an adult that allowed one to innocently touch a friend without worrying about all the repercussions?

Or perhaps there were repercussions. When they were together, Claire noticed little things that made her heart pick up speed. An appreciative sweep. A lingering touch. An undercurrent of longing.

Chapter Fifteen: Claire

She would have to be without senses to not pick up on Ryan's attraction, but as he'd made no definite romantic moves, she wasn't confident his feelings ran below the surface.

And with the future of the park looming between them, she wasn't sure she wanted them to. If they, *hypothetically*, started dating, she might feel pressured to give in to his desire to sell. Or, on the flip side, if he relented to her, she might be accused – by no one but herself, probably – of using her womanly wiles on him. And that was *not* the woman she wanted to be.

Then, there was the fact that he lived in Nashville. Even if the park closed, she would never move from her beloved island. Nor was she interested in long-distance. If ever she entered another relationship, she wanted it to be 'the one.'

This is all foolishness. I'm letting myself get distracted by unfulfilled wishes and a man who is too attractive for his own good. The tall, dark, and handsome type was overrated, and hazel eyes that promised a world of romantic possibilities were too expensive for her taste – like the Moonstone, nice to look at but dangerous to possess.

* * *

"Claire, we have a situation at the Widow's Walk," squawked the ride operator. Jack was out for the afternoon, leaving her in charge. "And it's pretty bad."

Great. "I'll be right there."

The scene at the haunted house was worse than Claire could have imagined. A sopping wet middle-aged woman stood out front, wrapped in a towel and weeping uncontrollably. The man next to her, her husband, Claire assumed, was pointing a finger at one of her employees and yelling obscenities. She broke into a run, coming between the two.

Do I Look Amused?

"Sir, sir! I'm one of the owners of the Pony Island Amusement Park. Please tell me what's going on."

Turning on her, the man did a double take. Guess he wasn't expecting a little lady in vintage clothes…OH! *The red hair.* Claire swept her ruby locks over her shoulder, glad the man stopped shouting.

"I'm here to help," she said, holding out her palms. "Now, what happened?"

The man's face colored as crimson as her hair. "Your ride almost killed my wife!"

"Pardon?" Claire blurted. Catching herself, she filtered her next words. "The Widow's Walk is a gentle boat ride. We've never had any problems before."

"It's terrifying!" the woman wailed. "Positively terrifying!"

"But what happened?"

"She jumped out of the boat," her employee said.

The husband growled, his hulking presence reminding Claire of a grizzly bear. "My wife FELL out of your sorry excuse of a boat into the filthy water. She could've drowned!"

"I'm sorry, sir," Claire replied. "If she was following the rules, that should not have happened."

"Are you saying it's MY fault?" the wife shrieked. Her husband flexed his meaty arms, but Claire refused to be intimidated.

"I need to see the tapes. Excuse me."

Leaving her poor employee with the hornet-mad couple, Claire jogged to the booth. The ride operator ran the tape back, confirming that the woman screamed and jumped to her feet before scrambling out of the boat. She missed the nearby platform and landed in the water. Claire watched several times to make sure, but it was indisputably the woman's doing.

"What am I going to do?" she asked aloud.

"That man's crazy if he thinks he can sue us," the ride operator said.

Chapter Fifteen: Claire

"People sue for much less nowadays and win. I've got to sort this out before it hits the news, or worse, social media."

Back with the couple, Claire prayed for fortitude. By the hate-filled countenance of the husband, she was going to need it.

"After reviewing the footage, ma'am, I'm afraid you were in violation of…"

"Are you blind?" her husband interrupted. "She fell! This is YOUR fault. We're going to sue!"

"You have no grounds! Our tapes clearly show…"

He poked his finger in her face. "I'll have your pathetic little park for breakfast. C'mon, babe. Let's go."

Claire hurried after them, panic seizing her. "You can't do this! We didn't do anything wrong!"

He ignored her, stalking to the exit with his wife jogging in tow. Claire stopped in the middle of the pathway.

"Get out, and never come back! It's people like you who ruin things for everyone else!"

As soon as the words were out, she regretted them. Guests stared at her open-mouthed. Parents clutched their children. With a sob, she bolted toward the nearest employee gate. *How am I going to fix this?*

Backstage, she called Mr. Dunlap and explained the situation to him. After urging her to make a copy of the tape immediately, he let her go with a warning.

"I'll have my staff prepare for the worst, but with social media, people can do far more damage than ever before. Let's hope no one caught your outburst on camera."

"I know. Thanks, Mr. Dunlap."

* * *

"I've never met a broken heart my peach cake couldn't soothe," Miss

Hattie said, setting a plate on the restaurant's kitchen table. "Sit down, sugar, and tell me what happened."

As she drowned her sorrows in fruity heaven, Claire spilled her guts to her mentor and friend. Miss Hattie listened until the end, reserving her comments until she'd heard it all.

"My, my, Claire. You let loose, didn't you?"

"I'm mortified, Miss Hattie! I'm stressed about the park, but that's no excuse. No matter how awful a guest is, we're supposed to treat them with respect." She plunked her forehead down on her arms. "What am I going to do if they sue? Everyone in the park has a cell phone. Someone probably caught my outburst on camera."

"If they did, they did," she replied. "You're human, child."

"I know, but…"

"Claire, listen. Anyone who's been on the Widow's Walk knows you don't fall out of one of those boats unless either you jump or someone pushes you." The older woman patted her gently. "I could be wrong, but it's likely nothing will come of this. People get upset over all kinds of things, but most realize how foolish they've been once the moment has passed."

"I hope you're right," Claire replied. "Time will tell."

Chapter Sixteen: Claire

Pony Island boasted one grocery store, local and family-owned. 99.9% of the goods were ferried in from the mainland, and the prices were raised to compensate. Claire kept to a strict budget, favoring family recipes and simple dishes. Tonight, she was making her favorite comfort food. Homemade meatloaf with cream cheese mashed potatoes, and sautéed garlic green beans. Her mouth watered as she gathered ingredients, soothing some of her anxiety.

"Hey there."

She spun from the store's selection of potatoes – russet and red – to find Ryan right behind her. He appeared to have run all the way from the park, his sweat-soaked shirt clinging to his…

"Hi!" she blurted. "What are you doing here…at the market?" *Oh, boy.* "You're grabbing dinner, aren't you?"

Ryan's cheeks behind his beard darkened. "Actually, I was looking for you."

Is it hot in here, or is it just me?

"Were you running all over town?"

"No, I had help. This," he pointed to his toned…heart, "is from the log flume."

"Oh." *Why, oh, why can't I stop staring?* The side of his mouth tipped up. She whirled back to the studs…spuds…potatoes. *Arg!* "What do you want?"

"I have news."

"You could've texted, or even called. You know, no one calls anyone anymore. What's up with that?"

Ryan turned her back around, resting his warm hands on her upper arms. Goosebumps sprouted like daisies.

"What's this?" he asked, trailing his fingers over the bumps as if they were Braille letters. She shivered.

"Stop! You're freaking me out."

"Hm." He dropped his hands to his sides, killing all of her fantasies about being romanced amongst the produce. "I heard about what happened."

"Oh."

"But I have good news. I spoke with the couple on the way out…" *Oh no…* "And the husband retracted his statements."

"What?!" The few people in the store jumped at her outburst. Pulling Ryan away from the spuds, she stopped in an empty aisle. "What? How? I'm speechless."

"I guess by the time he reached the gate, he'd let off enough steam. I intercepted him, and we worked things out." He nudged her arm. "He even asked me to apologize to you."

She pursed her lips. "I find that hard to believe."

"Well…it took a little persuasion. Man to man."

"Ah. I see. *Man* to man."

Ryan took great interest in his tennis shoes. "Sorry, Claire."

"No, it's fine. I get it." She sighed. "I guess I'd feel the same. Men tend to understand men, and women tend to understand women. I wish I'd handled it better, though."

"I heard about that, Donald."

Chapter Sixteen: Claire

"Quack." She leaned back against the boxed cereals. "Thanks. I owe you one."

"How about dinner?" He bent over her basket, bringing him near enough for Claire to catch a hint of his spicy cologne. "Whatcha making?"

"Meatloaf."

"Meatloaf?" He retreated with a grimace. "Maybe another time, then."

"What? You don't like meatloaf?"

"My grandmother always put green bell peppers in hers. I hated it!"

"Mine is amazing," she said, preening. "No peppers."

"Then count me in."

"You want to come to dinner…at my house…tonight?"

He looked both ways before leaning in. "Are you planning to poison me?"

"Do you think I would tell you?" Her traitorous eyes darted to his mouth…so close. His perfect lips formed a devastating smile, and she couldn't so much as blink.

"I'll be there," he whispered, his spearmint breath kissing her cheek.

"What time?"

"Six," *gulp*, "thirty."

"See you then."

As she gathered the rest of her groceries, one thought kept her sane. *We won't be alone.*

* * *

"Sweetheart," Natalie began, her skilled hands deftly peeling potatoes, "I have an announcement."

Claire paused over her own spud to analyze her mom. Ever since Natalie arrived at the keeper's cottage an hour ago, Claire had been venting about her own day, skipping over her crush in the cereal aisle. She must have been high on sugar fumes to wish she was kissing Ryan. *Did I even think to ask my mom about her day?*

"Sorry, Mom. I've been going on like a runaway train. What's up?"

"Jack took me out to eat last night, and…" Natalie wiped her hands on a damp dish towel. When she pulled a velvet box out of her pocket, Claire squealed.

"Did you say yes?"

"I did," Natalie replied, revealing a sparkling emerald surrounded by diamonds, "on the condition that you approve."

"Of course I do! Didn't Jack tell you he asked me first?" Claire waved to the ring. "Put it on, Mom!"

Natalie posed as Claire *ooh*ed and *aah*ed. Once the ring was safely stowed, they went back to peeling.

"We talked for a long time last night," her mom said. "We want to get married at our engagement party."

"Why not call it a wedding, then?" Claire asked, puzzled.

"Jack doesn't want to tell his kids ahead of time that our engagement party is also our wedding."

"Why? They love you. I'd think they'd be thrilled."

Natalie shrugged. "For one, his son and daughter-in-law are having financial and marital problems. They would feel obligated to help, and he doesn't want to add to their plate. He's also concerned about his children's reaction if they knew we plan on a short engagement. Even though their mom's death was over two years ago, they're still grieving. Jack was more prepared, being with her through all the treatments. He feels it's better to rip off the Band-Aid. I can't say I understand it, but he knows them better than I do, and I trust him."

"That's sweet, Mom."

"That's not all." Her mom set down her paring knife. "Would you be my maid of honor?"

Chapter Sixteen: Claire

"Oh! I would love to, but I assumed you would ask Helene. Does this have to do with Mr. Lanier's passing?"

"No," Natalie replied. "I'd already decided. It would mean everything to have my favorite girl next to me."

Claire wiped a tear with the back of her hand. "I would be honored, Mom."

Grasping hands, they shared a moment. When they broke apart, Natalie's mind switched to planning mode.

"If you're ready, First Mate, I'm going to put you to work."

"That's why you asked me. You need a lackey!"

"You caught me!"

Laughing, Claire scooped the last of the diced potatoes into the pot and went to rinse them in the sink. "Then, I'm in your service, Captain!"

As she filled the pot with water and put it on the stove, sprinkling as liberally with salt as she did her pasta water, her mom brought several bags in from her golf cart.

"I did some shopping today. Wanna see?"

"Yes, yes, yes!" Claire replied, clapping. Wedding bells might not be in her future, but she would do her best to give her mom the best second wedding in the history of second marriages. She couldn't think of a more deserving bride. Jack was one lucky man.

When Natalie left around 6:15, Claire cleaned up and picked a dress that enhanced her eyes and showed off her figure...*not that Ryan's joining the party has anything to do with the wardrobe change.* She smoothed her hands over her hips as she checked her reflection in the floor-length mirror one last time. Her heart played like a drumline.

"What am I doing? He's going to know this is for him. I should change."

The doorbell rang. *Too late.*

Chapter Seventeen: Ryan

Ryan had never thought of cereal as the food of love, but their tête-à-tête in the breakfast aisle said otherwise. Perhaps he should have brought Lucky Charms instead of the bouquet of pink anemones he'd picked up at the island florist.

When he arrived in his mom's golf cart, another stood out front of the stone keeper's cottage. He'd never seen Claire driving one – she preferred her bicycle – but it was logical she would have an alternate form of transportation for bad weather or grocery shopping. The lighthouse was quite a ways from everything else.

Built in the early 1800s, the old Pony Island keeper's cottage had been bought by Claire's parents. They spent years restoring it, raising Claire at the same time. It was no wonder she loved old things.

The current light tower, a 1908 construction built to replace the crumbling original, was retained by the Coast Guard until the light was moved the decade before they were born. Claire and her parents fixed the space into a fun hangout for her and her friends. He had fond memories of playing epic Sorry! with the gang before his crush and coveting Mancala games with Claire after his crush while his brother and Kendra flirted over Battleship. Not that Ryan ever *let* her win.

Chapter Seventeen: Ryan

Tamping down his butterflies, he passed through the familiar flower garden, climbed the worn stone steps, and knocked on the fire engine red front door. *What am I thinking, inviting myself over for dinner? I never do things like that.* But the temptation of spending the evening alone with Claire, even over meatloaf, was too good to resist. Before he could knock a second time, the door was opened by the Beast himself.

"Who are you?" the burly man asked, eyeing Ryan as if he were a mounted insect.

"Ryan," he replied, bristling. The man was like a lion on vacation, with his bushy blond hair and beard, Hawaiian shirt, khakis, and leather sandals. Claire had definitely not mentioned a visiting boyfriend. *Was this guy her type...or is she being held hostage by tacky burglars?* "Who are you?"

"Grant Whitlow, a *friend* of Claire's." The way the man emphasized 'friend' set Ryan's teeth on edge. He bulked up his own frame. He was no scrawny weakling himself.

"May I speak with Claire?"

Grant eyeballed him up and down like a bouncer, crossing his hairy, tree-trunk arms over his pro-wrestler's chest. "We were about to sit down to dinner. Not sure the lady wants to be disturbed."

What is this? Claire's way of humiliating me? Ryan's retort was cut off by giggling in the background. He peeked around Grant to find Claire snickering with another woman who looked vaguely familiar.

"That's enough, honey," the woman said. "Come on in, Ryan."

The Beast slapped him on the back. "Sorry about that, man. The ladies put me up to it. If there's one thing I've learned in ten years of marriage, it's to play along with my wife's schemes."

In the cozy foyer, Grant's wife stepped forward with a shy wave. "Do you remember me? Amie Harper, back then?"

Memories of a summer long ago flooded back. They shared a hug. "Amie, how are you?"

"Doing well." She patted her husband's chest. "We have two kids, but they're playing at a friend's house tonight."

"Dinner's ready," Claire said, motioning the couple to pass her. Ryan hung back, the bouquet dangling loose at his side. "Are you coming?"

"Why didn't you tell me you were having company?" he hissed. "I was kidding. I didn't intend to butt in."

She released the anemones from his grasp and paused to admire them as he drank her in. Dressed in a soft powder blue dress with a limp bow at the base of the 'V' neck, she rivaled Lauren Bacall, his grandmother's favorite actress. Her fading hair fell in soft waves and was accented with a white flower on one side. One lock strayed from the rest, curling over her shoulder.

"They're lovely. Thank you, Ryan."

As are you, he thought, but the words wedged in his throat. The color of her dress brought out her eyes, two whirlpools threatening to drown him. Sailing closer to the rocks, he smoothed back that pesky strand, relishing in the silky-softness of her hair. Claire sucked in a breath.

"Are you sure I'm welcome?" he whispered, resting his palm on her shoulder. "I don't want to intrude."

"Please stay. I've made plenty," she replied, her plea reverberating in the small space. The ruby stain on her upturned mouth flashed like the tower's old light. *Stay clear or drown!*

But drowning looks perfect right now.

"Hurry up, you two," Grant called. "We're hungry!"

Claire snapped into action. "I should put these in water. I'll be right there."

Ryan corralled his emotions before entering the dining room. Kissing Claire would not magically make their problems go away; it would create more, namely, the breaking of both of their hearts.

* * *

Chapter Seventeen: Ryan

"Where have you been keeping yourself, Ryan?" Amie asked. "We come to our vacation home every summer, and we've never seen you around."

"I moved to Nashville after college. I was offered a job with a large commercial real estate firm, and I was happy enough with city life that I decided to stay. My best friend from college, Dominic, runs a foundation that raises money for MS, so I help out with it too. We're in the middle of planning our yearly 5K at the moment."

"Wonderful cause! How long are you here for?" Grant asked, eating half of a buttered roll in one bite.

Ryan exchanged a look with Claire. "A couple of weeks. We have some things to work out with the park before I leave."

When the kitchen telephone rang, Claire jumped up to answer it. Ryan and the Whitlows shared memories from Amie's summer internship and things the family enjoyed doing on the island. Outside of the park, beachcombing was a favorite.

"And our daughter adores the ponies," Amie said. "She wants to go into equine medicine someday."

"She wants to be a vet?" Ryan asked.

"Horse doctor," Grant replied with a laugh. "She's very specific."

Claire appeared in the doorway, breathless and smiling. She looked at him, not their friends.

Play it cool, man.

"Guess what?"

"What?" Ryan asked, resting his elbow on the table.

"That was Wish Granted." She did a little dance. "Their next monthly winner chose a day at our park as their wish! They'll be bringing the child, parents, and siblings, along with a TV crew. Not only is it an honor to be chosen, it'll be great publicity!"

Amie was the first up for a hug. "That's wonderful, Claire! I'm thrilled!"

"Awesome, girl!" Grant said, giving her a side hug. "When's the big day?"

"They haven't set a date yet. Kendra will get with them."

Ryan was already on his feet, but he wasn't sure what to do. Would she accept a hug? Should he give her a hug? And in front of the Whitlows?

You're overthinking this, he told himself, pulling her into the world's quickest side hug. She deflated like an old balloon.

"What do we need to do?" he asked, feeling the rift between them widen. Lifting her chin, he encouraged her to look him in the eye. "I'm here for this…for you."

"Thanks, Ryan." She wrung her hands. "I'm not sure. I'll have to think about it. Right now, though, let's finish eating. I have a lemon icebox pie that's waiting to be devoured."

"With meringue?" Ryan asked, hopeful.

"Your grandmother's recipe," she replied, appearing to gauge his reaction.

"You're amazing," he said, willing her to feel the force behind his words.

And I could kiss you.

Chapter Eighteen: Ryan

The Whitlows left around nine. As Ryan helped clean up, Claire washed the dishes the old-fashioned way. He picked up a towel and started to dry.

"They make dishwashers, you know," he said, putting a dry plate in the cabinet.

"They don't clean near as well as these two hands." She rinsed a skillet and handed it to him. "Sorry for not telling you about Amie and Grant...and for asking Grant to intimidate you."

"I deserved it." He nudged her shoulder before moving away. "Dinner was delicious. Thank you."

"Are you a meatloaf convert?"

"I concede. You've won me over. And those mashed potatoes? Mmm!"

When he returned to her side, she bumped him with her hip. Intrigued, he stared at her a second too long. She threw a wink in with the bargain.

"They're killer, aren't they? I expect the coma to hit right about... now."

As a matter of fact, he did feel a little sleepy. He made a show of yawning. She finished the last dish and waved him off.

"Let it air dry. You need to get on the road."

"Are you kicking me out?" he asked, not ready to end the evening now that they were finally alone. The kitchen clock ticked in the silence.

"It's a clear night," she conceded, pulling out packets of hot chocolate mix. "We could check out the view from the tower."

He filled the kettle while she dug out toppings. *Dinner, dishes, hot chocolate...Claire.* The simple routine struck him with the feeling of home. *I could get used to this.*

"Tell me about Dominic's foundation," she said as they waited for the water to heat. "You haven't mentioned it."

"I haven't?" He mimicked her cross-armed stance across the island. "His brother Michael was diagnosed with MS while they were in high school. Dominic's the type who can't sit by and watch, so he started raising money, first to help his family, and second, for research. Michael's March grew from there, and now, we have an annual 5K in the fall."

"I love that, Ryan," she replied, leaning on the granite. "You work with them too?"

"On a voluntary basis. I handle the budget for the marathon." He wrapped his hands around the edge of the counter. "I also help on the ground as needed."

Claire stiffened. *She's putting two and two together. 'Reasons Ryan needs to leave ASAP.'*

"I'm sure there's a lot to do," she said. "We put on a lot of events at the park, and I always feel like I'm forgetting something."

"Then, you need a *slack guy*. I'm Michael's March's official go-getter, do-this-er, and move-that-er. Whatever they need."

"Sounds like you've found your place." The kettle's whistle cut the thick air. She poured the water, her back to him. "A slack guy, huh? I reckon your brother thinks he's ours."

Chapter Eighteen: Ryan

Right. You're not needed, Ryan, except in name only.

Carrying two cups laced with whipped cream, they climbed up, up, up the spiral staircase to Claire's reading room. She flipped on a lamp to reveal the familiar curved bookcases, assorted floor pillows, and a couple of cozy chairs. A glass door led out to the balcony.

"This is the first time we've been up here alone," he said, Claire's hot cocoa-flavored truth serum loosening his tongue, "the first time in our lives it's just the two of us. With Travis and Kendra around all the time, you and I never spent much time together," he leaned his head back against the cushion, "even though I wanted to."

"I never knew you did." Her expression was shrouded in shadows, and he couldn't read her tone. "You should've said something."

"It would've looked weird," he replied, shrugging. He tried to laugh, but it came out more as a snort. "Teen guys don't try to be alone with a girl unless they like them, right? Travis would've been all over me."

Gusts whistled through leaks in the glass as his mixed signals hung in the air.

"You're probably right."

She didn't return the sentiment, making him wish he'd kept his mouth shut. He needed to change the subject, and fast.

"Wish Granted, huh? That's great! Is this the first time?"

"It is. Jack's daughter is on the board now, so I don't know if that's a conflict of interest, but I assume the child picked us of their own volition."

"I'm here for whatever you need." He was surprised to find her frowning at him. "What?"

"The park's an amazing place, Ryan. I wish I could help you see that."

"I do see that."

"Do you? This child could go anywhere in the state – Hilton Head, Charleston, Myrtle Beach – but they chose Pony Island. There's magic here." As she scooted forward in her seat, she glowed from within.

"Our park is more than entertainment. It's a storehouse of childhood dreams, precious moments, and lasting memories. If what we have makes even one person's life better, it's worth all the sacrifice."

If she'd been collecting for public broadcasting, he'd be broke. He didn't respond, but at that moment, a secret wish was born in his heart. Maybe the park was worth trying to save, no matter the cost.

"Shall we check out the view?" he asked after a moment's silence. She rose without speaking, and as they made their way outside, he rested his hand on the small of her back.

They stayed like that, gazing over the dark Atlantic waters, counting ships and constellations. He itched to pull her into his arms, but now wasn't the time for romantic notions. More serious things loomed on the horizon.

When her cell pinged, she pulled back from the railing. He let his hand drop, intending to give her privacy, but he was captured by the name on the screen.

"Lugosi? Who in the world do you know named Lugosi?" he asked. She clutched the device to her chest, the whites of her eyes bright in the moonlight.

"No one."

Wait. The text message below the name is mine.

"Let me see that," he said. She relinquished control with a deep sigh. "Why does that name sound familiar? No, don't tell me."

"Oh, come on, Ryan!" She crooked her fingers by her canines.

No way! Dracula? He grabbed her about the waist, nuzzling his face into her neck as she giggled madly.

"I *vant* to suck your blood!" A second later, he heard *thunk, thunk, thunk!* Claire cried out and jerked toward the railing. A flash caught his eye. "Oh no!"

Her cell flipped end over end until it landed in the grass.

"Ryan!"

Chapter Eighteen: Ryan

"Stop, Claire," he said as she started for the door. "It's my fault. I'll go."

He kicked himself on the entire jog down the spiral staircase. At the bottom, dizzy though he was, he stopped only a second to recalibrate. He could smell Claire's essence – sea and sunshine. If she hadn't dropped her phone, there's no telling where that scene would've gone. *Stupid phone. Stupid me. Stupid phone!*

Outside on the lawn, he turned on his cell's flashlight, scanning the seagrasses for the wreckage. How would a smartphone fare in a 150-foot drop? At least, the grass was tall and soft. *As long as it didn't hit a rock.*

A gleam bounced back at him. Ryan pounced on the phone like a cat and pushed a button. Immediately, the screen lit up, showing a missed call. Turning it over, he was delighted to find Claire's device none the worse for wear as far as he could tell. He moved out where he could see her leaning over the railing and waved her lit screen.

"Found it!" The sea drowned out her answer. "Wait there! I'm coming up."

Inside, he paused in the lean-to, noticing a wedding magazine marked with neon Post-It Notes. *Claire is getting married? To who?!*

"Hey!" she said, barely huffing from her own speedy descent. "Is it dead?"

"No, none the worse for wear." When he handed it over, he didn't allow his hand to linger. If she was engaged, he didn't want to make more of a fool of himself than he already had. Oblivious, she checked her device over. "I'm awful sorry, Claire."

"Don't worry about it." She wrinkled her nose. "At least it didn't tumble into the water."

"That would've been bad." He propped his hands on his hips, his chest constricting. *Why hasn't someone said something? What if I'd kissed her?* It was his party all over again. He was the same stupid, lovesick fool, blind to her interest in another man. "I should go."

"Ryan, I promise I'm not upset. It was an accident, anyway."

"It's late, Claire." When he started from the room, she surprised him by grabbing his arm in a death grip.

"Please don't leave upset. I'd never forgive myself if something happened."

Feeling trapped, he pulled out the only card he held. "Your fiancé won't like me being here this late."

"My fiancé? What are you talking about?"

"The wedding magazine," he said, pointing. "Why didn't you tell me?"

"Oh!" She shook her head until the flower threatened to wobble off. "That's not mine, Ryan. My mom and Jack are engaged. She asked me to be her maid of honor."

"Your mom and Jack?"

She nodded, her lips curving up. "Yes. I'm not even in a relationship."

"That's great…I mean…your mom's marrying again. That's…wow. How do you feel about that?" He wrapped his arms around himself to keep from hugging her.

"I'm happy for her, and he's a great guy. It was time."

"Good." *Way to go, idiot, making assumptions.* When he got home, he was going to bang his head into the wall. "It's late, though. I'd better let you get your beauty sleep." *Not that you need it, you gorgeous, adorable, very single woman.*

Claire led him back through the kitchen to the front door. "Mom gave me a *long* list of things that need to be done…like I'm her daughter or something. Want to help?"

"I'd be happy to." *That scored me points.* "Thank you for dinner. It was," he gave a chef's kiss, "perfection."

As he putted away, he kept the image of Claire backlit by the open door in his mind. If ever there was a sight worth coming home to, that was it.

Chapter Nineteen: Claire

"You and I never spent much time together, even though I wanted to."

He liked me.

"Teen guys don't try to be alone with a girl unless they like them, right?"

He didn't like me.

Claire, stop plucking the metaphorical daisy!

She relived the moment Ryan grabbed her – before her cell went hurtling toward the ocean – over and over, dwelling on the intimacy of the silly moment. What would have happened if she hadn't been such a klutz? Would the hug have turned into a cuddle, the nuzzle into a kiss? Did she want them to?

What was going on between them? They were bound together by a rubber band, pushing apart one day and springing back together the next.

The Wish Granted call struck a chord with Ryan, but it wasn't enough. As the organization was state level, not national, the TV coverage would only go so far, mostly to people who already knew of the park's existence. Plus, the focus would be on the child – as it should be – not the venue.

Donning a cheerful apple green blouse and a berry pink swing skirt, she left home feeling anything but. Spending time with Ryan again after all these years – make that *joined at the hip* – was taking its toll on her heart.

I mean, how cute is a man drying your dishes?

If Ryan's heart was pricked by Wish Granted, maybe *showing* him the park from a different perspective was the key. It was worth a try. Stopping at an overlook, she texted him to meet her at the train station around 9 am.

Claire: And I'm changing your ID in my contacts. No more Dracula.

Ryan: Don't you dare!

Ryan: Unless it's something like Clark Kent or Peter Parker.

Claire: Superman or Spiderman, eh? I remember you as a Batman fan.

Ryan: I'm over the Dark Knight and fancy gadgets. I need a superpower.

Claire: How about Clark, then? He's a classic, created right before World War II. Plus, Lois Lane has amazing style.

When Ryan didn't respond, she pedaled on, regretting every nanosecond the reference to the Man of Steel's girlfriend. *Will he think I'm flirting? Am I flirting?*

* * *

The Pony Island Express Train, or PIE Train, as it was known, was a steam locomotive their grandparents imported from England in the 1960s. Having carried loads of children away from the London Blitz before being scrapped for parts, the rescued engine was the perfect choice for an amusement park. After undergoing a loving restoration and multiple refurbishments, Old PIE was as beloved as an old dog.

Ryan stood on the platform when she arrived, wearing a blue shirt,

Chapter Nineteen: Claire

a size too small, emblazoned with a red 'S'. As soon as he saw her, he struck the iconic superhero pose, stretching the bounds of the faded cotton. As if on cue, the train whistled.

"You didn't!" Claire cried, doubling over. "Where did you get that shirt?"

"I dug it out of my old closet," he replied, reddening. "It's a little snug."

"It's perfect." She carefully wiped away a tear, avoiding another mascara disaster. They boarded one of the open-air cars, choosing a seat at the back. "Come to think of it, I think I remember it. You wore it on the youth group trip to Charleston, the one where Amanda Portland kept sitting next to you."

"Don't remind me. I tried to pass her off to Travis, but that made things worse."

"Is that why I don't remember you wearing it again?"

"No." He clenched and unclenched his hands, looking out toward the park.

The engineer called, "All aboard," before receiving the all-clear from the stationmaster.

"I never wore it again," Ryan said, "because of you."

"Me? What did I do?" She held on to the seat as the train lurched to a start. Ryan shifted to hook his arm over the back of the bench.

"I overheard you telling Chad Berry you didn't like superheroes." He smoothed his thumb over some flaking paint. "You thought they were stupid."

"I did?" She clamped her hand over her mouth, recalling the persistent flirt with a cringe. "I'm so sorry! I thought he had a crush on me, and I only said that to get him to leave me alone."

The train reached its max speed as it passed behind some shrubberies, and the breeze cooled Claire's stress sweat. Who else's life had her casual comments messed with? No, she refused to go down that rabbit hole. What was past was past.

"Feel free to geek out now," she continued, pointing to her own unusual style. "You won't be alone."

Ryan wasn't secretive about his perusal, laying his arm behind her, not quite touching. He appeared to be weighing his words.

"You've always stood out, Claire, vintage or not, but I think this look suits you. You have an old soul."

"Thanks, I think."

He nodded once. "It was a compliment...Lois."

As the train pulled into the first stop, she forced her warm cheeks away from her handsome companion and his tempting flirtation. From this point on, the park would unfold before them. She was determined not to let Ryan off the train without sharing everything she loved about her Pony Island Park.

"Did you know the first Ferris wheel was built for the 1893 World's Fair in Chicago?" Claire asked Ryan as the Sand Dollar came into view. *His arm is mighty distracting!* "While ours is much smaller, it offers an amazing view. You can see both the mainland and the ocean."

"Uh-huh," Ryan said, studiously observing the rainbow swings going round and round. "I'm aware."

"I wasn't sure you noticed. You were more interested in Gabby Finch than the view."

"You're wrong," he replied, touching her shoulder with his thumb. "Gabby wanted to ask me if Colin Burgess liked her. Nothing happened."

She gave him the side-eye. "Even when you got stuck for half an hour?"

"I didn't know you were paying attention to my whereabouts," he said, snuggling his arm a little closer. "I remember you and Jake Louis pairing up for the Whirlpool...more than once."

"As friends," she corrected.

"That's not what Jake thought."

Chapter Nineteen: Claire

"He was wrong." Craning her neck as they passed the Sand Dollar, she continued. "I had a crush on someone else, but I don't think he ever knew."

Ryan tensed, and his voice came out a whisper. "Who?"

"I'm not telling! It's past anyhow."

"Yeah, it's past." He brushed her arm with the backs of his fingers, drawing out goosebumps. "Tell me."

"No! And if you don't stop tickling me..."

"Sorry." But not sorry enough to move away. She shivered with pleasure, and Ryan took note, pulling her all the way into port.

"You weren't the only one with a crush, Claire Hensley."

Neither spoke as they passed the Widow's Walk. She didn't want to spoil the mood by asking him why he stood her up, and it appeared he wasn't going to be forthcoming. That too would remain buried in the past.

"Did you know," she said, nodding toward the empty stage, "that our humble park hosted some of the biggest acts from the 1940s during our first 20 years? And that our summer camp talent shows ran every year from 1952 to 2011, except for 1983 and 19...94."

"I did." He repositioned, taking his arm with him, and pointed to Piper's. "Did you know Miss Hattie has worked here since she was sixteen? She created her amazing peach cake recipe in 1970, sealing her position forever."

"I did." She felt her blush to her roots. "I'm sorry, Ryan. I assumed you didn't notice stuff like that."

"Cause I'm a guy," he asked, "or because I've been pushing to sell?"

"The latter." The train arrived back at the main station. "Our history is one of the things I love about Pony Island. I thought if I reminded you, it might sway you."

He gripped the seat back in front of them in preparation for their exit, his body pivoting to face her. "Claire, please don't think I proposed selling because I don't appreciate the park. It's an amazing place."

"But?"

At that moment, the safe-to-exit whistle blew. He followed her across the platform and down the steps, his expression impassive. They paused in the walkway.

"Let's table this discussion until after the Wish Granted visit," he said. She pressed her fingers to her temples.

"That gives us more time, anyway."

"What's next on your agenda?"

"Paperwork."

He shoved his hands in his pockets. "Wanna grab lunch later?"

"Can't. I've got a conference call at 11:00, and I'm not sure how long it'll go."

A pair of pretty college-aged girls in trendy attire walked by, eyeing Ryan like he was a chocolate fondue fountain. He caught them staring and politely returned their smiles.

"How about dinner?" he asked, looking back at Claire.

"Why? So you can wear me down?" she spat. "Is that what all this is about?"

"All what? You're the one who invited me on a memory-laced train ride tour," he countered. "I think you owe me a listen."

"I don't owe you anything, bud. I'll see you later." She spun on her heels, but he cut in front of her.

"No, you don't. I'm asking you to dinner because I enjoy spending time with you. Is that so hard to believe?"

"Kind of! If Travis inherited your dad's share of the park, would you have given me a second thought before running back to Nashville?"

When the vein in his temple pulsed, she wanted to kick herself. *What a low blow!* But before she could make amends, he spoke, his words clipped.

"My feelings toward you are separate and apart from the fate of the

Chapter Nineteen: Claire

park. No matter what *we* decide, I will always choose to remain friends. You may feel differently."

Friends. Claire let his words settle as she debated what to say. He hadn't confirmed any romantic notions, even though the man sure knew how to get a girl's hopes up. Neither had he mentioned staying on the island – a definite deal-breaker. She should steer clear at all costs.

"I've got to go to the Beachcomber to settle Mom's wedding menu. That was going to be my dinner." She clasped her hands behind her back. "I'd love a wingman."

"How about," he mimed ripping off a button-up shirt, "Superman?"

"Perfect."

Chapter Twenty: Claire

The Beachcomber Bakery & Café was 'the' spot on the island for breakfast and lunch, but recently, the owners added a light dinner menu. Natalie and Jack, wanting to support the new venture, asked them to cater the reception. As Claire and Ryan walked to the restaurant, her tongue tingled at the prospect of cheesy bacon grit cakes drizzled with sweet and spicy sauce. *The South meets Asian fusion.* And then dipped in the whole mustard aioli? *Can. Not. Wait!*

"Have you been back to the café during your visit?" she asked, interlacing her fingers at her stomach. "They've created some fun, innovative dishes."

"Not for dinner. Mom and I went for brunch the other day," Ryan replied.

She couldn't resist another glance at his sleek grey linen suit, his shirt open-collar. *Talk about spicy!* The man could put on anything and come out as delectable as a bacon-wrapped jalapeno. She smoothed her hand over her rumpled skirt. And she was a pile of dirty laundry. *Lovely.*

When their arms brushed, she jumped to the top of the Lighthouse. Ryan, suave as ever, crooked his elbow. All – *er, let's be honest, Claire*

Chapter Twenty: Claire

– *most* thoughts of cheesy bacon grit cakes fled as she searched for adjectives to describe the feel of his muscles. Manly? Firm? Sculpted?

"Even at day's end, you look nice," he said. "I had to shower and change. How do you do it?"

"I was thinking the opposite," she replied, trying to smooth her skirt again. "Rumpled and disheveled, more like. You look very nice, though."

"Nice, hah." She caught the nervous hitch. "We sure know how to throw around compliments. I should've said," she held her breath, "beautiful."

She'd never been more grateful for her cerebellum. *Ryan thinks I'm beautiful?* He chuckled at her bass-mouthed expression.

"Was that really so shocking?"

"I reckon it was," she replied, tucking her hair behind her ear. "If I return that with, you look very handsome, will it go to your head?"

"Definitely." They were nearly to the café when he spoke again. "I assumed you'd heard that a thousand times over. Don't tell me I'm the first."

"No, my daddy beat you to it," she winked, "but thank you."

He flexed under her hand, tempting her fingers into an appreciative caress. *Strapping – that's the one.* Another flex told her he'd noticed. He stepped up their pace as they approached a little garden between the buildings, the pineapple guava shrub hiding the perfect nook for a clandestine kiss.

But he didn't stop, and soon, they were conversing with the maître d'. She resisted the urge to bolt. What was going on between them, and how would it affect their working relationship?

"A special spot for a special girl," the owner of the Beachcomber said, escorting them to the patio. "And Ryan, it's so good to see you. How long are you here for?"

"A couple weeks," he replied, keeping it simple. "Claire tells me the new dinner menu is to die for."

"I wouldn't go that far – we try to keep out of the murder business – but we're upping our game to compete with the fare on the mainland."

Ryan pulled out Claire's chair, his fingers brushing her shoulders as he pushed her in. They ordered two glasses of mango lemonade and sat back to wait for the small plates. An epic view of the ocean spread before them, white caps crashing in the distance, gulls swooping for dinner nearer the beach.

"I've always been thankful I wasn't born a crab," Ryan said, his bearded chin propped in his hand. "Too dangerous." Before Claire could chime in, his phone buzzed. "Sorry. It's Dominic. Do you mind?"

"Go ahead."

Ryan remained in his seat. "Hey, buddy. What's up?"

Claire focused on the ocean, her lemonade, and the clouds, but it was impossible not to hear one half of the conversation.

"No, I haven't checked my email for a couple hours."

I love the rustle of the palmetto fronds. It's kind of like a maraca. Cha-cha-cha!

"Uh-huh."

Why is our state beverage milk? *Are there a lot of cows on the mainland?*

"I get that, but..."

The horizon is so straight! I wonder how far I can see.

"They canceled?" Ryan pushed his fingers into his hair. "You weren't kidding when you said it was a disaster!"

He's taking this personally. Michael's March means something to him.

"I'll do what I can, but that kind of thing is easier in person."

And you're stuck here.

"Okay. Talk later."

She let Ryan process in silence, knowing her questions wouldn't help. A couple of minutes later, he spoke, his voice rising with each sentence.

"Tri-Star Barbeque backed out of the event. They've provided food

Chapter Twenty: Claire

for the 'Patient and Family Dinner' for the past five years at a reduced rate. People come from states away solely for their smoked pork. They're a Michael's March institution!"

"Why did they cancel?"

"Rising supply costs. I understand, I do, but we can't afford to pay full price."

"And you don't want to put that burden on your guests," she concluded. "I know how that is." He tapped his phone on his palm in full thought mode. "What's the plan, then?"

"I've got to find a new caterer...in budget...from 600 miles away." He scratched his chin. "Kinda hard to do taste tests."

"Why don't you call up some of your favorite restaurants?"

"I'm a single guy with high rent and a low budget, Claire. I'm usually hitting drive-throughs or ordering pizza, if I eat out at all."

The waiter served two trays worth of appetizers, mains, and sides, all of which smelled incredible.

"You haven't taken a date somewhere like this?" Claire asked, waving toward the spread. "I love this kind of thing – fusion dishes, small plates, comfort food with a twist. I'm sure your guests would too."

"No," he said with a smolder to rival Flynn Rider's, "not like this."

Her foot brushed his leg – *accidentally* – and his eyebrows shot up like a pair of firecrackers.

"Small table," she muttered, pinning her legs under her chair. "Why doesn't Dominic handle it?"

Ryan picked up a grilled scallop skewer dripping with garlic-lime oil. "He's on a strict training diet. Too much temptation. Plus, I'm much more trustworthy with finances. He pays first and checks the bill later."

"Gotcha. What will you do, then?"

"All I can do. Ask for recommendations and hope for the best."

She reached for the coveted grit cake, cracking it open to reveal steaming cheese and smoky bacon. Dipping a chunk in mustard aioli, she prepared for a trip to culinary paradise as the bite touched her lips.

"Speaking of temptation," Ryan said, husky as roasted corn, "*that looks delicious.*"

Chapter Twenty-One: Claire

The sun wasn't due to set for another hour. Claire knew she should head home, but she wasn't ready to leave Ryan's company. By the way he hung about her like a moth at a lamppost, it seemed he felt the same…or perhaps, he had something to say about selling the park. He paid for dessert, despite her reminder that it was a 'working' meal and her idea. Was he trying to 'wine & dine' her into his way of thinking?

"I left my bike at the park," she said, clasping her hands firmly in front of her.

"What a coincidence," Ryan replied, suddenly shy. "I did too. I, uh, was hoping we might take a ride after dinner, since you have to bike home anyway."

"That sounds nice."

They started off, the foot between them a gray zone of touch-or-no-touch. When he didn't offer, she stuck her hands in her pockets. No need making a fool of herself.

Ryan's bike was the same one from high school, bringing a flood of memories. He peeled off his jacket and stowed it in her basket before rolling up his sleeves, revealing his brace-free wrist. As they wheeled out of town, he gave a hoot, kicking his feet out.

"It's been ages since I've ridden a bike. I forgot how much I missed it."

"Careful there, bud," she said, swinging out of the way and zooming ahead. "You're lookin' a little rusty."

Pumping his legs, he soon caught up. "Just you wait, Hensley. It's coming back."

"It's true, then, what they say? You never forget how to ride a bike?"

"Nope." He flashed a grin. "Like I never forgot…this island. I know it like the back of my hand."

He sounded like he'd nearly let something slip, or it could have been the inch-thick branch he rolled over. *Stop it, Claire! We're not kids anymore.* She couldn't analyze Ryan's every word and action. The crush that his return reignited needed to be snuffed out before she fell hard. Maybe a change of subject…

"I don't know if you've noticed, and I'm not trying to gossip, but…"

"What?" he asked.

"Kendra's been acting odd lately." They rounded a bend. "She gets off her phone when she sees me coming, hides text messages, doesn't return calls and texts as quickly. I'm worried."

Passing the lighthouse, they decided on a full loop before sunset. A herd of ponies grazed ahead, and they pulled to a stop. Ryan took a long swig from his water bottle before offering it to her.

"Sorry. I don't have cooties, though," he said, "if you're thirsty."

She wiped the spout first, as if that would define their non-dating status once and for all. Out of the corner of her eye, she could see him watching her like a lion hunting a prized gazelle. She snapped the top down and held it out.

"Thank you."

He wrapped his hand around hers. "Don't mention it."

Thankfully, the ponies moved out of the road. She spotted the foal

Chapter Twenty-One: Claire

as they passed, but before she could mention it, Ryan spoke.

"Travis has been stressed lately, but I don't know anything. Mom's worried too."

"I'm sure he misses your dad."

"We all do, but this is different. He said he was 'frustrated.' Kendra too."

"Do you think it has something to do with the park? Maybe they're worried about their jobs. Why won't they talk about it?"

"Maybe," he replied, "but I don't think so. Who knows? It could be health-related, or they might be thinking of moving off the island. I'm sure they'll tell us when they're ready."

"Health? Moving?" She careened into an overlook and screeched to a halt. He circled back and hopped off his bike. "Both of those are huge, Ryan! Why wouldn't they want us to know? We could help. We could pray. We could…"

"Claire," he said, covering her hands on her handlebars, "they'll tell us when they're ready. I know my brother. You know Kendra. They're private people but not to the point of shutting us out completely. Trust them."

She exhaled before prying her fingers loose. "You're right. I'm overthinking again. I tend to do that."

"Let's watch the sunset," he said, offering his hand.

Nothing prepared her for the sensation of holding Ryan's hand for the first time. Warm and a little gritty, it brought forth images of Fourth of July picnics and Friday night football games, summers in the water and bonfires on the beach. At the railing, he pulled her to his side, not letting go.

Neither spoke as the sun kissed the horizon, washing the mainland in a glory of orange and gold. A zephyr whipped around them, tussling her hair and fluttering the collar of her blouse. Ryan tucked her hair behind her ears.

"Between the wind and the sunset," he said, trailing his thumbs along her jawline, "I feel like that prince who finds a mermaid bending over him...right before she swims away."

Talk about mixed signals. Was he trying to be romantic or not? That thought perished as he brushed his thumb over her bottom lip, tilting her head one way and his, the other. Pressing her hands to his chest, she felt his heart galloping like the island ponies. Could he feel her pulse too, the thundering of a thousand hooves?

"Give me one good reason," he whispered, touching his nose to hers, "why I shouldn't kiss you right now."

She gripped the soft cotton of his shirt like a lifeline, ready to pounce in desperation. How many times had she dreamed of this moment, falling asleep with a kiss to her pillow? After how many winning football games did she wish for him to swoop her down like the sailor in Times Square? Stolen kisses on the beach, atop the lighthouse, on every ride in the park. As a teen, she imagined each scenario with a hope unrivaled.

"Ryan..." Then, as thunder comes after lightning, his hesitation was finally clear. *Right before she swims away.* Right before *I leave*. He wasn't staying. "You're the one who leaves," she said, pulling out of reach, "not me."

Breathing hard, he leaned against the railing, his face toward the final rays of the sun. "We'd better get a move on."

At her door, they said a stiff goodbye. Inside, she distracted herself by checking an unread text message.

Jacob: Sorry, Miss Claire. I've got the summer flu. I'll be out for a few days.

Claire: Oh no! I hope you feel better soon!

As she headed into her bedroom to change into her coziest pajamas, it hit her. With Jacob out, there was one person slated to wear the Sea-Horse suit.

Chapter Twenty-One: Claire

"Great."

Chapter Twenty-Two: Ryan

"Idiot! Idiot! Idiot!" Ryan pounded out with each dribble of the basketball. When he went for a layup, the drat ball bounced off the rim and sailed into the dark street in front of his mom's house. As he chased it down, the contrast between noisy Nashville and the quiet peace of the island echoed in his ears. He could hear the waves splashing on the nearby shore, not the revving of engines. The rustle of the wind in the palm trees, not the slamming of apartment doors.

He wiped his face on the hem of his t-shirt before heading in. He'd probably annoyed their long-time neighbor, Mrs. Richmond, enough for the night.

Basketball was his dad's thing, taking the brothers on every Saturday morning while their mom made waffles, pancakes, or on special occasions, the most mouthwatering cinnamon rolls. As little kids, he coached them in the basics, patiently running after every ball bounced off the rim. When they were older, he schooled them in the finer points of the game, the tips and tricks.

While Ryan enjoyed basketball, football was his favorite sport. Travis was the one who stuck with hoops and helped the Pony Island High team make it to regionals two years in a row. Their dad never played

Chapter Twenty-Two: Ryan

favorites, though, cheering as hard for Ryan as for Travis. Ryan could hear him now:

We only have one life. Whatever you do, give it your best. And never forget, boys: I'm proud of you.

"I really miss you, Dad. I'm trying to figure this out, the park...and Claire. I wish you were here. I could use your advice right about now."

His mom was in bed, it being well after ten. While he was way too old for a curfew, he found himself sneaking past her room to grab fresh shorts and a tee. A quick shower would help him relax. Then, he'd try to get back into that spy novel a friend back home recommended...

Back home. In Nashville. Had the Tennessee capital become *home* for him? Honestly, he hadn't thought about it. It's where he landed his first job. It's where he earned his paycheck. It's where his cookie-cutter apartment sat. Sure, Dominic and his family were there too, but they had their own lives. He couldn't hang with them *all* the time.

Had he ever hung those pictures his mom bought? Or were they in the guestroom closet? What did it say that he didn't remember?

Yet here on the island, Claire was making a life for herself. The park wasn't a 'workplace.' Her position wasn't a 'job.' Her unique house was filled with lifelong memories and carefully curated items that were an extension of her. Being in her home was like getting a giant Claire hug.

Don't go there, Ryan!

But stupid him, he had gone there...and if he didn't watch it, he would be right back, a dog begging for more. Like an addict, once reconnected, he couldn't get enough of her. The barriers of their teenage years were long gone, replaced by this yo-yo of emotions neither seemed able to control.

She wants me, but only if I stay. If I quit my job and risk everything on our dying park. If I make all the sacrifices.

The water ran cold with his heart. *Is she trying to manipulate me? Seduce me, figuratively speaking, into seeing things her way? Are her affections irrevocably tied to the fate of Pony Island?*

After midnight, in the murky state between awake and asleep, a memory emerged. He was in tenth grade, and Claire, Kendra, and Travis were in ninth. Two days prior, Kendra broke her foot playing softball and was in a wheelchair. Ryan wanted to ride the Eye of the Hurricane, but Travis, nursing a massive crush, wouldn't leave Kendra. Claire volunteered in his stead.

Inside the dark vault, he and Claire left a person's space between them as they leaned against the carpeted wall.

"You nervous?" he asked as the ride started spinning.

"Uh, *no*," she replied, turning her face toward him. Her light blonde hair was short that summer, brushing her jawline. Why he noticed, he wasn't sure.

Dork. Duh, she's not nervous. "Me neither."

They fought against the centrifugal force, pushing their way higher up the wall, trying to outdo each other. He managed to shift about forty-five degrees when something pressed over his hand. The Gravitron was at max force. Turning his head? Impossible. But he knew what it was.

Claire's hand. Is touching. Mine. We are (almost) holding hands.

First came the heart palpitations. Then, the cold sweat. His brain struggled with this new software. **Claire 1.0** was not installed, and his hardware kept misfiring. Questions pinged back and forth like his dad's old *Pong* game.

Ping. Why is Claire touching me?

Pong. What does it mean?

Ping. Does she realize she's doing it?

Pong. Does she like me?

As the ride eased to a halt, her hand fled.

Game Over. You Lose.

He knew he preferred racing games. One track. One speed

Chapter Twenty-Two: Ryan

(superfast). One finish line.

Neither spoke as they escaped from the Hurricane. They didn't make eye contact for days. Not until weeks later did things return to pseudo-normal – with one huge adjustment. Ryan's teen heart was hopelessly in love with Claire Hensley. No other girl would ever do. As he finally drifted off to sleep, one question lingered. *What if I'd stayed?*

* * *

The peacock took care of breaking the ice the next morning.

"Reynaldo, get off of Harvey!" Claire was yelling when Ryan happened upon her. He followed her focus to the mascot of the Seagull Scrambler. "How did you even get up there?"

"Better question," he asked, sidling up, "how are you getting him down?"

"Peacocks are supposed to fly as high as eight feet," she muttered, putting her hands to her cheeks. "Harvey's at least fifteen. How did he...?"

A maintenance worker scrambled out of the bushes behind the giant seagull, flapping wildly. "There's a ledge back here that's about six feet tall. Maybe he flew up there before climbing up Harvey's back. There's an awful lot of scratch marks."

"Highly plausible," Ryan said. Claire whirled on him.

"How am *I* getting him down? He's *our* problem, Ryan Lanier!" Her flames burned from more than Reynaldo's antics. "Unless you sell out, we're in this together."

"No bird wrestling for me, ma'am." He showed off his brace-free wrist and leaned within inches of those cherry bomb lips. "I'll be cheering..."

"From the nosebleed, if you're not careful," she interrupted, huffing.

"What's with you anyway, Mr. Hot-and-Cold? Last night, you almost…" she looked around before hissing, "kissed me. Now, you're…"

"Go get your bird," he replied, dropping back with a wink. "I'm your wingman, remember?"

"Whatever." She rolled her eyes, but her delight wreaked havoc with his pulse. Flirting with Claire was like getting a shot of dopamine of a morning. The more he got of the 'happy hormone,' the more he wanted…but that meant staying on the island.

Claire called for the scissor lift, and soon, Reynaldo was safely on the ground. As the peacock strutted off to share his exploits with his harem, the wind whipped up. Ryan spotted dark clouds on the horizon.

"A storm's blowin' up," Claire said, her arms wrapped around her torso. "We may have to close early." Her voice caught. "Kendra scheduled the Wish Granted visit for tomorrow. I hope we don't get too much damage."

His spirits sagged with her shoulders. "We'll do the best we can."

"*We?*" She hiccup-snorted. "As long as you're here. Someday soon, you're leaving. Then, it'll be *me*…if I have anything left."

"Pony Island isn't everything, Claire. There's a whole world to explore."

"Maybe not to you. I've never known anything else." She checked her watch. "I've got to go. See you later."

He let her leave without a word. The sooner they figured out what to do, the better.

Chapter Twenty-Three: Ryan

"How was Mom this morning?" Travis asked when the brothers met for a break. Ryan motioned toward the Rolling Waves coaster.

"She was smiling when I left." They entered the queue behind a group of young teens. "I don't think she's sleeping well, but everyone says to give her time."

"They were married for thirty-five years. I can imagine."

"Keep me posted when I go back to Nashville," Ryan said. "I'll call Mom more often now, but she won't want me to worry."

"Will do." They moved forward. "Change of topic. What's up with you and Claire?"

Ryan folded his arms across his chest. "Nothing's up. We're trying to figure out what to do about the park."

"That's not what it looks like from where Kendra and I are standing. More like watching a fireworks show over the ocean."

Ryan snorted. "Hardly."

Travis was quiet as they loaded themselves into the seat behind the kids. "Have you ever thought of moving back? It's not the same without you, Bro."

Do I Look Amused?

"I have a solid job, Trav. I'm moving up the ladder."

"There are jobs in South Carolina too." The ride creaked up the big hill, but the anxiety twisting Ryan's gut had nothing to do with the 130-foot drop. Before he could muster another excuse, Travis continued. "Sorry, man. I shouldn't be butting in, but we miss you, 'kay?"

"I miss y'all too."

Conversation was impossible as the car crested the hill, dropping down, down, down before swooping up, over, and around. Ryan held up his arms, trying to enjoy it, but inside, his thoughts mimicked the coaster's path. As they exited the ride, he had no answer.

* * *

They closed the gates at noon, and within the next half hour, the entire crew evacuated. Ryan was on his way out when he noticed a light on in the office. Inside, he found Claire hunched over her computer.

"What are you doing here?" he asked. "Everyone else went home."

"I'm as safe here as there," she replied, squinting at the screen. "It's not a hurricane. Might as well get some work done while the place is quiet." He plopped into a chair, earning a frown. "You don't have to stay."

"I'm not leaving you here alone." He pulled up his browser. "Pretend I'm not here."

A couple of minutes passed, filled with intermittent typing and rain pelting the windows, before she flopped back in her chair with a *huff*.

"I can't think with you sitting there."

He switched to the other chair. "Is this better?"

"No."

He sat cross-legged on the floor and peered over her desk. "How about now?"

"No! Get up, Ryan." The lights flickered, shutting down her

Chapter Twenty-Three: Ryan

amusement. She did the same with her computer. "We may lose power anyway."

Rising with a cat-like stretch, she motioned to the closet. Inside, he found a prepper-strength emergency kit. Pillows, blankets, and flashlights, to name a few. As he checked one of the flashlights, the overhead lights went out.

"Right on time," he said, holding the light under his chin. "Boo!"

"Hilarious. Hand me one. I, uh…"

"No explanation needed."

While Claire was gone to the restroom and a walkthrough of the office, he got an idea. A brilliant, awful, *fantastic* idea. He was adding the finishing touches when she returned.

"Ryan?" He popped his head out as she squealed, "A blanket fort!"

Her happy dance made it all worthwhile.

"Come on in. I have snacks."

Four chairs formed the corners of the fort, a large patchwork quilt muffling the storm outside. Additional quilts padded the thin office carpet. In the middle, he placed an electric lantern. She helped him arrange the pillows.

"Did you raid the vending machine?" she asked, eyeing the pile under one of the chairs.

"Yes, ma'am. I wanted to be prepared for all cravings." He held up salted pretzels and peanut butter M&M's. "The perfect combo. Sweet and salty."

She reached past him for a pack of Twizzlers. "I haven't had these in forever! Want one?"

"Why not?"

They chewed in thoughtful silence for a moment before the lump in his throat threatened to choke him more than the red licorice.

"I'm sorry, Claire. Yesterday was…"

"It was you."

"Pardon?"

She twirled her half-eaten strawberry rope, snagging a bite. "The guy I had a crush on. It was you."

"I had no idea," he replied, losing his appetite, "but the feeling was mutual."

"I gathered that." The fake flame flickered off her downturned face. "I checked into UT Knoxville for college before you left, but I ended up going with an online program."

"Not because of me, I hope."

"Only a little. I knew I wanted to work here, so it seemed silly to leave for three or four years. I had everything I needed here." *Ouch.* She continued. "I dated some. There was one summer intern." When she fanned herself, he rolled his eyes. "We thought we were in love, practically engaged, but when he asked me to go home with him, I couldn't bring myself to leave."

"Guess it wasn't love," he replied, watching her reaction. She held eye contact for a moment.

"No. After that, here and there, but eligible men are hard to come by around here."

"Eligible men, eh?" he repeated, laying back on some pillows. "You sound like Jane Austen. Twelfth-grade English, if you're wondering."

She rearranged her skirt after propping herself on her own pillows. "What about you? Nashville must be brimming with…"

"Eligible women? Ha, I suppose. I dated a little in college, but nothing stuck. Since then, a few women from church. Nothing serious." He swallowed. "I've been focused on my career, and that doesn't attract the women I'd be interested in."

She was curious, but the questions didn't escape. He let the topic die. The romance of the tent was tempered with the ruin of the day prior, but that was for the best. He wasn't sure he could withstand the hormonal barrage of being trapped alone with Claire for hours

Chapter Twenty-Three: Ryan

otherwise.

"You know, I have some leftover fries from Piper's in the fridge," she said. "Want some?"

"Cold?"

At that moment, he detected the low hum of electricity. She rose to her knees.

"The generator started a while ago, but it provides minimal power."

"Why didn't you say something sooner?" he asked, crawling out behind her.

"And ruin our heart to heart? No way!" She leaned back against her office door, her hand on the knob, as he moved in close.

"Open the door, Claire."

"One sec." She laid a finger on his sternum. "I have *one* cup of fry sauce. Will that be a problem?"

He pushed gently against her touch. "Open the door, Claire."

"First, I need to know," she traced her finger to the base of his breastbone, "do you double dip your fries?"

Why, oh, why is she flirting now, and over fry sauce? He removed her hand before he went crazy, resisting the urge to interlace their fingers.

"We shared a water bottle yesterday. I'm sure we'll survive," he said, growling. "Now, open the door."

She stared up at him, snapping out of some kind of trance. Without a word, they headed to the kitchen and scraped up a decent dinner, including a second cup of undipped fry sauce. Back in the tent, by silent agreement, they stuck to neutral topics – like which boy band's reunion they would rather attend – until the storm outside blew over. Actually, that turned into a debate. Who knew their teen preferences ran so deep?

Inside, however, Ryan and Claire were caught in the eye...the eerie calm before the final blow. Would their friendship survive this storm?

The scene outside was better than they could've hoped, mostly broken limbs and a couple of overturned trash cans. Claire called their maintenance crew to assess for further damage and get things cleaned up.

Ryan found himself with a black trash bag and a mechanical claw picker-upper thing making his way around the Carou-Sail, cherishing the moment she revealed her crush and chastising himself for wanting to kiss her again. When would he get off this crazy ride?

He caught a glimpse of Claire, cute in her teal dress and yellow tennis shoes, laughing at something a workman said. She was one in a million. *Am I crazy to want off?*

Chapter Twenty-Four: Claire

"We have here the owners of the Pony Island Amusement Park," the interviewer said, pushing a microphone under Claire's nose. "Miss Hensley, how did you feel when you heard that nine-year-old cancer patient Mikayla Mendez chose Pony Island as her 'wish destination'?"

"Thrilled!" Claire replied, willing her happy vibes through the camera to potential guests. "She is such a sweet girl, and we're honored by her choice. Our crew is on hand to make sure her day is as perfect as can be."

The middle-aged woman turned to Ryan. "Mr. Lanier…"

"Call me Ryan," he replied, sending the interviewer into a twitter.

"Ryan, you've recently inherited from your father. You have our deepest sympathies."

"Thank you."

"The park's financial troubles are no secret. I guess what we're all wondering is, what do you see in the park's future?"

Nothing was decided. Would he use this public opportunity to plead his case? She fidgeted with her charm bracelet until she felt his hand on the small of her back.

"We're taking things one day at a time," he said, pressing her side gently. "Claire and I have been friends since childhood. I'm sure we both want what's best for Pony Island."

"Spoken like a true diplomat," the woman replied, shoving the microphone back at Claire. "Do you have any final words for our viewers?"

Claire froze, her vocal cords tied in a knot. *What if we have to close the park? What if this is the only Wish Granted visit? What if I lose everything?*

"We're open for the rest of the season," Ryan said, unruffled, "and we intend to make this the best one ever. Y'all come on out and see us!"

As soon as the cameras were off, he hustled her back to the crew area and shoved a water bottle into her hand.

"Breathe, Claire. Take small sips. It's going to be all right."

Taking a long swig, she came up choking. He snagged a pile of napkins from the crew cart and patted her back until she calmed.

"How can you say that?" she asked, wiping her cheeks. Black smudges marred the thin white paper. *Stupid mascara. Before Ryan, I didn't have this problem!* "We're about to lose everything!"

Instead of arguing, he pulled her into a boa constrictor wrap, threatening to squeeze out all of her worries by sheer force. Oxytocin, the 'cuddle hormone,' tried to overcome her, but she refused to cry in his embrace. He was the cause of all her stress!

"We'll figure this out, honey," he whispered, stroking her hair. "Nothing has to be decided today."

"You keep saying that." When she struggled, he let her pull back enough to look up at him. "One day will have to be the day, Ryan. And this," she gestured between them, "isn't helping us decide."

"I know." He released her and stepped back. "I'm sorry. I can't seem to keep my hands off you."

"Oh, shut up. I know what you're doing."

"What's that?" he asked, danger swirling in his hazels.

Chapter Twenty-Four: Claire

"Claire! There you are," Kendra said, jogging from the crew gate. "You're up."

Hooking her best friend's arm, Claire escaped with a wave. She hadn't told Ryan about Jacob's illness, and she didn't intend to. The last thing she needed was his flirty comments when she was wearing fifty pounds of faux fur and sequins. She'd never survive.

* * *

"Look, Mikayla," the girl's mom said. "It's the Sea-Horse!"

Claire knelt down as gingerly as possible and spread her hooves wide. The small girl, wearing a mermaid scale headscarf and an oversized Wish Granted tee, clamored into the kelpie's hug.

"I love you, Sea-Horse!" she squealed, squeezing tight. "I sleep with one of your babies every night."

Babies?

"She has a stuffed Sea-Horse from a previous visit," her dad explained. "Hardly leaves her side. Thing's practically worn out."

Claire burst to speak, but it wasn't in the Sea-Horse's character. Good old Kendra received her telepathic message.

"Please let her choose a brother or sister from the shop, our gift." *Go Kendra! Such a thoughtful touch, brother or sister.*

When the dad protested, Mikayla's mom stepped in. "Thank you very much. She will love that."

By this point, Mikayla had buried herself in the costume's shoulder, her little face nuzzled between the head and the body. Claire could hear her super-soft whispers.

"I was so excited when Mommy told me we were coming to see you. I love you so much! I wish you could come home with me."

I do too, sweetheart. I do too, Claire thought, willing in vain for her tears not to fall. A moment later, Mikayla's mom coaxed her away.

A strong arm helped Claire stand. She was about to turn toward the person she assumed was Ryan when through the kelpie's mesh eyes, she saw Kendra's expression. Her best friend watched Mikayla and her parents make their way with the film crew toward the Carou-Sail, the girl's favorite ride, with damp cheeks and a wistful smile.

"That was beautiful." Claire had instructed Kendra not to reveal her identity around Ryan, so instead of escorting her back to the crew area, the traitor walked off with a wave. "See y'all later!"

Great.

"So, Jacob," Ryan said, "have you asked her out yet?"

Huh? Ryan took 'Jacob's' silence as dissent.

"Come on, man. Clock's ticking." He nudged her arm. "I'm pretty sure she's interested. What's the hang-up?"

Had Jacob confided in Ryan about his crush on Morgan? Claire gave a massive shrug.

"Look, dude. It's your decision, but the truth is, I let the girl of my dreams go without a fight. I don't want to see you making the same mistake."

She could see his hangdog expression through the mesh. *He's talking about me, right? Was I truly the girl of his dreams? Then, why did he leave without telling me?*

Had any hope of a second chance been swallowed by the Nashville Predators? *What?* Her dad had been a hockey fan. She'd heard of them.

"Hey, do you need help getting that thing off?" Ryan asked. Claire almost flopped back on her shiny tail! In response, she swung the horse head back and forth. "I've got to meet up with Claire soon. Catch you later!"

He stuck his fist out, and after a second, Claire returned the gesture with a 'hoof' bump. As soon as he turned away, she galloped out of there. Once she was clear of the costume, she washed her face in the crew restroom and snuck out to her bike. She had a meet-up to ditch.

Chapter Twenty-Five: Claire

Clark: Where are you?

Claire shoved her phone in the back pocket of her old jeans. She hoped her contemporary outfit, complete with a bleached Carolina Panthers t-shirt, a baseball cap, and huge shades would be inconspicuous in case Ryan came to town searching for her. Was she overreacting? Yes. *But that man...* They needed space before they ended up lip-locked in the nearest closet. If he wasn't staying, kisses would be a prelude to heartbreak.

Ding, ding! She locked her front door with a jerk. "Leave me alone, Ryan."

Weddings were a pretty big thing on the island, so it was no wonder the florist carried a wide array of flowers as well as decorations that could be either rented or bought. Claire headed there in her golf cart to check on some things for her mom.

Inside, the heady floral fragrance hit her like a brick. It was such a strong contrast to the fresh scent of the ocean. Could she ever leave the island for the mainland? Never...at least not forever. She was a thalassophile, a lover of the sea, a *mermaid*. The ocean *was* her blood.

"Claire, is that you?" the shopkeeper called. "I didn't recognize you in that get-up."

"Yes, ma'am," she replied, hanging her sunglasses on her collar. "I came about my mom's order."

The woman frowned. "Oh, dear. I left a message for Natalie, but she hasn't called back. I wasn't able to get the purple delphiniums from my supplier. Is there something else your mom would like?"

"Oh no! She had her heart set on those. Uh, I'm not sure. Flowers aren't my specialty. Let me ask her."

When she unlocked her screen, she saw three messages from Ryan.

Clark: You said to meet at the gate, right?
Clark: Kendra said you left already. Are you mad at me?
Clark: Can we talk about this?

Instead of responding, she called her mom and got her voicemail.

"I'm sorry," Claire said to the shopkeeper. "Could we get back to you on this?"

"Unfortunately, I need to know now. I won't be able to get a replacement otherwise." She swept her arm out toward the store. "Now, if there's anything here she would like, that shouldn't be a problem."

Claire scanned the room and spotted some purple foxgloves. A memory tickled her subconscious, but before she could second-guess herself, she said, "She likes foxgloves, and they're similar. Let's go with those."

With that done, she squared away the rented decorations and left to change back into her normal clothes.

Heh, she thought, putting on her tailored skirt and blouse, *I guess normal is what we get used to.*

* * *

By the end of the afternoon session, Claire was sweating buckets. She'd forgotten – somehow – how draining wearing the suit was. It wasn't

Chapter Twenty-Five: Claire

like they could afford a climate-controlled suit like Mickey Mouse. If she didn't get it off soon, she was going to shrivel up like a raisin.

"My turn," yelled a snotty five-year-old boy. He wrapped his arms around the Sea-Horse's tail, AKA Claire's legs, and started jumping up…and down…and up…and down. Claire flailed her hooves, praying she wasn't about to tumble over with a kiddo in tow. The last thing they needed was an angry parent.

"Whoa, buddy," said Ryan's voice, steadying her. As soon as his arms came around her torso, he froze.

He knows I'm not Jacob.

Ryan righted her and removed his hands, probably fearing he'd manhandled a teen girl, as the boy's parents escorted him away screaming.

"I'm sorry," Ryan said. "Are you all right?"

The jig is up.

"Yeah," she replied, heading toward the gate. "Thanks for saving me. Now, help me get this thing off."

Ryan didn't respond as he followed her, fending off eager guests. In the crew area, she lifted the horse's head and sucked in fresh air. How did Jacob stand that stale aroma day in, day out? *Yuck!*

Once she was clear of the suit, she plopped down on a bench, fanning herself with her hand. Ryan offered her a cold bottle of water and eased down next to her.

"I didn't know you were on suit duty this afternoon."

"I was." She took a drink. *Please don't ask about the morning session.* "Jacob got sick."

Was that a lie? No, but her stomach squirmed all the same.

"Can I pour this over my head?" she asked, lifting the bottle. "That thing is suffocating."

His focus dropped to her crew-issue t-shirt, amused, before bouncing back up. "Be my guest. I won't look."

Cold water splashed out of the bottle as she jerked it down. "Forget I said that!"

"Too late," he replied, grinning up at the cloudless sky.

"Ryan!" Rising, she held out her hand to pull him up. "Help me get this thing back to wardrobe?"

Instead, he tugged her down to eye level. She braced against the back of the bench while he held her hand captive.

"I texted you."

"I know. I'm sorry for not responding. I was…confused."

He looked as if he wanted to say something else, but exhaling, he broke eye contact. "Please say you're not mad at me."

"I'm not mad."

"We need to talk."

And I need air. She eased her hand away and stood upright.

"There's nothing to talk about. We want two different things in life. Unless that changes…"

She turned away. The chasm between them threatened to consume her, body and soul.

"What hold does this island have on you, Claire? I love it too, but I can come and go. It's like you're…"

Trapped?

"Say it, Ryan!"

"Afraid…afraid to leave, like if you do, it won't be here when you get back."

"That's ridiculous! I've left before."

"For a week or two at the most. Then, you always come back." He rested his hand on her shoulder. "Honey, talk to me."

"I'm not your 'honey,' Ryan!" She spun on him, knocking his arm away. "I'm not *your* anything. You made that decision ten years ago."

"A decision I've regretted ever since." He gave her a significant look. "As you know."

Chapter Twenty-Five: Claire

He must have guessed the truth about this morning.

"But not enough to come back," she spat. "We're going in circles, Ryan. Drop it already! We're not meant to be. Not back then, and not now." She scooped up the limp kelpie.

"Don't say that," he pleaded, pulling the horse head from her load. "We can make this work."

"Don't even suggest long-distance! I'm not going there."

"I can't up and quit my job, Claire! I have obligations."

"But you're asking *me* to?" She sped up to a trot. "What a hypocrite!"

"No!"

Dumping the costume at wardrobe, she closed herself in a dressing room to change out of her tee and shorts. Ryan waited outside, probably trying to come up with a tempting negotiation. At least, he hadn't kissed her. She didn't need *that* kind of temptation.

After dry shampooing her sweaty, now-pink hair, she felt ready to face the opposing army. Ryan stood at the ready, but the sag of his shoulders almost made her wave the white flag. Eyes closed, she held her face to the sea breeze, willing it to soothe her frazzled nerves.

"I'm not asking you to give all this up," he said off to her right. "Just wishing you'd give us a chance, even if it meant…"

"Leaving?"

"If you had to to be with me." How he worked up the courage to touch her arm, she didn't know. When she didn't pull away, he further endangered himself by slipping his arms around her waist from behind. His touch stirred her soul, his nose drawing a curve from her jaw to her temple. "Hopefully not forever."

"Ryan," she whispered, forcing out the terrible words, "stop. Please."

To her disappointment, he released her, and they made their way back to the public area. She pointed to the Dolphin Dive, desperate for a distraction.

"We have several rides to test. Wanna go?"

"Sure…" His cell rang, and when he saw the caller, he changed his tune. "Sorry. I've got to take this."

"Will you be at movie night?"

"Wouldn't miss it."

"We'll see about that," she whispered as the snake of jealousy bit her heart. *Who is Taylor? And are they male…or female?*

Chapter Twenty-Six: Ryan

"Thanks for letting me know, Taylor," Ryan said, rubbing his forehead. The bosses were lenient about his extended leave, but his coworker Taylor's call confirmed they wanted him back. He'd banked several weeks of leave, though, and he was prepared to take all of it if need be.

A quick check with Travis confirmed that Jacob was out sick that day. Why hadn't Claire told him she was on Sea-Horse duty or that she wasn't Jacob? It wasn't so much what he said, she already knew about his crush, as the fact she'd hidden her identity.

Did she think he would make fun of her? She should know him better than that. Was it about the money, not being able to hire another suit performer? He picked up an order of fried oysters and boiled peanuts, gorging himself on the comfort foods. Neither snack revealed any answers.

Okay, Lanier, he thought, savoring the salty overload, *maybe it's time to look at this from another angle. She likes me. That much is obvious. But I'm the enemy because I'm looking at everything in a logical, realistic way. As you do.*

Wrong! Not if I want to be on Claire's good side. Save the park, get the girl, right? So, how do we save the park?

They needed money to fix up the rides, but as Ryan scoped out the place after ten years of distance, he noticed other issues. Chipped paint, overgrown flower beds, underutilized spaces. These were things one might not notice when one saw them day after day, but guests certainly would. Maybe the first thing they needed to do was spruce up the place.

But that required manpower, which meant paying overtime. Which wasn't in the budget.

"And that's why we're stuck in this rut." He tapped the side of his thumb on the table. "We need a new source of income."

His greasy basket liner stared up at him, giving him an idea. He checked the schedules for Savannah, GA the next day before texting Claire with an invite. When she agreed, he did a happy dance. *Who doesn't love a food truck lunch?*

Updating the park's menus would be a good start, he thought. *If people see we're keeping up with the times, maybe we can catch some more customers.*

As long as Claire's nostalgia doesn't hold us back.

* * *

Drive-ins have nothing on Pony Island's Pictures at the Park, Ryan mused, enjoying the laid-back atmosphere of the after-hours event, *even if the crowd is a bit thin.*

A screen was set up on the stage, a projector at the ready. He'd hardly seen Claire, bustling about like a bee, but he did spy the popcorn stand. A free scoop in hand, he made his way to the back of the audience where their families gathered. His mom offered her extra seat. The knowing thickened his throat.

"Thanks, Mom," he said, settling into his dad's old folding chair. He reached for her hand. "What's playing tonight?"

Chapter Twenty-Six: Ryan

"*It's a Wonderful Life,*" she replied, wiping her cheek.

"Isn't that a Christmas movie?"

"Haven't you heard of Christmas in July?"

"It's June," he retorted, spotting Claire on the approach. Where she was going to sit became way more important than seasonal mix-ups. "Here, Claire, you can have my chair, if it's all right, Mom. I'll find another one."

"Certainly."

Claire waved him down. "No, I'll stand. I'm all over the place at these things anyway." She moved out of *but-I-insist* territory. He yearned to follow, but by her cold shoulder, he assumed it would be like chasing a seagull.

Edison bulbs strung overhead twinkled like bonus stars against the evening sky, filling the air with romance. Ryan slumped back as the movie started, whisking him away to Christmas 1946.

I bet Claire picked this movie.

Soon, he was swept up in the story, watching George Bailey sink to the depths of despair...*kinda know how that feels, buddy*...and laughing at the bumbling antics of the guardian angel Clarence...*that too.*

Claire drifted into his vision, her hand on her heart, a dream in her eyes. Ryan checked out the screen. All he saw was actor James Stewart in a suit and tie, his oiled hair mussed from all his troubles. *The dude looks like he's been run over by a Mack truck.*

But when Jimmy stuck a beat-up fedora on his head, Ryan felt, rather than saw, Claire's sigh.

Message received and noted.

* * *

They met at the dock at 9:00 the next morning. Ryan stumbled as she hopped off her vintage cruiser in a floral jumpsuit with knee-skimming shorts that fluttered in the breeze. *How does Claire always manage to look so stinkin' cute?* He hoped his blue polo and khaki shorts were up to par. It wasn't a date, but he desperately wanted it to become one. *Dress the part and all.*

With round sunglasses and a silk scarf tied around her hair, Claire was as picture-perfect as a movie star – *in need of a leading man.* Her graceful stride left him starstruck. She pulled off her sunglasses and gave him a once-over.

"You look nice."

"Nice? Ouch." He shoved his hands in his pockets for safety. "Unless that's a code word for something better. Like if I said you look 'nice' right now," he sidled closer, "that's not what I'd mean."

"And what would you mean?" she asked, smiling as she put the earpiece of her sunglasses between her natural, balm-only lips. He wanted to tug on his collar, but it was already loose. "Have I rendered you speechless, Ryan Lanier?"

The way she said his name made his palms itch. If she was going to flirt like this all the way to Savannah and back, he was a goner. *Too late.*

"Gorgeous, as always." He felt her bloom to the toes of his boat shoes. "Come on. Our charter's over there."

The captain started off as soon as they were ready. Claire wanted to stand by the outside railing, even though – or possibly *because* – conversation would be difficult. He settled with covertly observing her reactions to everything from the other boats, the swooping seagulls, and a serendipitous family of bottlenose dolphins.

"Look, Ryan!" she squealed, clutching his forearm and pointing like an excited six-year-old. "It's been forever since I saw dolphins up close. I hardly ever get off the island."

"I know," he replied, resisting the urge to touch her in return. "I'm glad you agreed to come."

"Me too. Thank you for inviting me."

Chapter Twenty-Six: Ryan

When they retired to the small lounge, he pulled up the Pony Island Amusement Park's website. The copyright date on the bottom read *2008*, and by the basic stock scheme, he was sure it was thrown together in a hurry and left for dead. Not that he would use those words when talking to Claire.

"I think our website could use an update."

Claire looked over his shoulder before taking a long sip of her ginger ale. "You're probably right, but that's not my area of expertise. Your brother set it up."

"I know, but he's not much of one for graphic design."

"Neither is Kendra or any of the regular crew, and we can't afford to hire a designer." She erased the condensation on her can with her thumb, water dripping over her lacquered nails. "As you know, it didn't used to be in the island curriculum, but it may be now. Everything's changed."

Ryan ran through the options. "What about one of the interns? Are any of them computer geeks?"

Claire appeared to think this through. "I think Jacob Hampton is in a computer club. Maybe he knows someone."

"Or maybe," he replied, hopeful, "he could do it. We can offer him a reasonable bonus, for both sides. It's worth a try."

"We can ask, but I always assumed he was more interested in computer games than programming."

"Maybe," Ryan said, tapping her can with his orange soda, "or maybe not."

Chapter Twenty-Seven: Ryan

Soon, they found themselves in the middle of Savannah's food truck haven, trying in vain to reduce their cravings to a reasonable amount. And by reasonable, he meant his daily spending limit. A day alone with Claire was worth every penny, and he intended to make it count.

"Ooo, Thai tacos," she said, nodding to a forest green truck. "That sounds interesting. Or grilled shrimp with peach chutney and Gruyere grits. Yum!"

"How about Southern-Italian?" he pointed out. "Deep-fried chicken ravioli with Tabasco marinara? I'm in."

"Barbeque pork and slaw...my heart! Oh, Tahitian chicken skewers, herbed couscous, and grilled vegetables. Yummy!"

"There's always pizza, which smells amazing!"

"Oh, Ryan, how are we ever going to choose?"

"I'm game for any and all. Let's do this!"

They started with their top choices – the barbeque and ravioli – and went from there. By the end of an hour, the table was littered with paper plates and crumbs. Ryan was stuffed tighter than a hog. Claire leaned back in her chair like she was about to fall asleep.

Chapter Twenty-Seven: Ryan

"That was amazing," she moaned, fingering the end of her scarf which she'd removed after departing the boat. Her pink hair was twisted up in a curious puzzle, revealing her slender neck. Perfect for kissing. Er...

"We're not scheduled to leave for a few hours," he said. "Want to explore a little?"

"Sure...if I can get up."

It was a decade and a half since Ryan's last visit to Savannah, so he was a little rusty. A local directed them to a quaint shopping street with boutiques, bakeries, and...

"The Bloomery?" he read on one sign. "What's that?"

"I would assume a florist," Claire replied, craning her head. "Yep. I see flowers."

"Aren't you a smart one?" he teased. She slipped her arm through his.

"And don't you forget it."

"I never have." Nervous, he reached for her hand. When her fingers interlaced with his, he wanted to break into song. Instead, he gave his inner self a mental fist bump. *Baby steps. Now, down to business.* "So, I have an idea for the park."

Her grip stiffened, so he gave her a gentle squeeze.

"What kind of idea?"

"One that, and I know this is a long shot, might boost our revenue."

"Shoot."

"I'd like to update our menus." When she didn't shoot him back, he continued. "We have some real winners. I don't want to touch those, but what do you think about doing some things like what we ate for lunch?"

"Food truck food?"

"Yeah." It terrified him that he couldn't see her expression behind her sunglasses as she thought it through. *Does she hate my idea?*

"I'm not sure how we would go about it..."

"Oh."

"But I like the idea. What exactly are you thinking?"

Inner fist pump! "International foods with a coastal-southern twist. We would start off with something easy and go from there."

"I'd hate to ask Miss Hattie to tackle that alone, though. Would we need to hire a chef?" she asked, frowning. "We can't afford that."

"Let's chew on it for a bit. Make some inquiries. Then, we'll decide."

Hoping to improve the mood, he searched for a good dessert option. They agreed on gourmet donuts, getting two to go. Strolling into a nearby park, he risked taking her hand again and was rewarded with a second chance.

A moment later, a kid on a skateboard knocked into him, making him drop his apple-cinnamon cruller.

"C'mon!" he cried. "Be careful!"

"Sorry, mister!" the boy yelled as he zoomed off.

"And now, I feel old." He threw away the remnant. "Guess I have to eat yours."

Claire giggled as he pretended to steal a bite of her chocolate-hazelnut, pulling it out of the way. "Maybe if you ask nicely."

"Fine," he replied, directing her into a shady grotto. "I think we're safe from tiny terrors here. Now, may I pretty please have a bite?"

"You may."

The threat of dripping chocolate crème made him hold her hand steady. Once her fingers touched his mouth, he pressed his thumb to her palm, rubbing circles as he barely tasted the concoction. Draping her arm over his shoulder, he tested the waters, one hand at her waist. She laid her palm on his heart, not pushing, not pulling, and closed her ocean blues.

"Are we doing this?" he whispered, his heart pounding like the surf. She bobbed her head once.

As a wave laps the shore was their first kiss, pure and gentle, but like

Chapter Twenty-Seven: Ryan

the tide before a storm, each surged stronger than the last. Claire's mouth was soft against his, dissolving his defenses. Her body became the ocean, and his, the moon. Ryan pressed his hand to her lower back, pulling her up on her tiptoes, and plunged into the deep.

* * *

Mayday! Mayday!
Man overboard!
Swimming to the surface, he put space between them, cradling her head with both hands. Their kisses calmed as they washed up on shore.
"That was..." he began, resting his forehead on hers.
"What have we done?" she blurted, breaking away. Her wide-eyed shock was like an Arctic wave. *She regrets kissing me already?* "Ryan! We can't do this!"
He wanted to retort, to ask 'why not?' but her terror stopped him. The answer was simple. *She may be attracted to me, like hydrogen to oxygen if that kiss was any indication, but that doesn't mean she wants a relationship.* Her deal-breaker was straightforward: no long-distance. And that was something he wasn't sure he should change, even if he wanted to.
Jobs on Pony Island, especially if the park tanked, weren't on the same level as his job in Nashville. Even getting one on the mainland would mean starting all over again. He had a great salary and good benefits: employer-provided health insurance, paid sick leave, and two weeks' vacation a year. Ownership of the park ensured none of that. He took his role as provider seriously, and if that meant leaving the island, she would have to be on board with that.
"Come on," he said, relenting for now. They both needed time to think. "We should get back to the charter, anyway."
They headed to the dock in silence, but inside, Ryan was reexamining.

This was his last chance with Claire. If he walked away now, there would be no next time. The door to her heart would be shut forever. His old feelings were back with a vengeance, and he wanted to believe they might have a shot at love.

But that would mean keeping the park, no matter the risk. Was it worth it?

Let's see how this plays out, he decided, stepping onto the boat, because the memory of her kiss said it was more than worth the risk.

Chapter Twenty-Eight: Claire

How can Ryan be so cool about this? Claire asked herself on the boat ride back. Her lips still tingled from his coarse beard, the sensation new and strangely addictive. *It's as if he kisses girls all the time.* She observed him behind her mirrored sunglasses, thankful for the World War II invention, and hoped it wasn't that. He'd never seemed like the philandering type, but if he liked her that much, why wasn't he willing to stay?

That's not fair. She stretched her legs out on the lounge chair. *He didn't come back expecting this, and I can't expect him to quit his job on a whim...but where do we go from here?*

The image of the Pushmi-Pullyu, the llama with fronts on both ends from *Doctor Dolittle*, the 1967 version with Rex Harrison – *you know, the doctor from* My Fair Lady – kept coming to mind. The park pushed them together, along with their apparently overwhelming attraction, but their life goals were too different, pulling them apart. Or at least what she assumed of his life goals. It wasn't as if she'd done much listening on that front.

I want him, but I don't want to want him. My heart broke when he left the first time. Can I fall in love only to lose him again?

I think it's a bit late for that, my dear, she chastised. *If he kissed you again, you know you'd kiss him right back.*

But what if he asked me to marry him?

Her inner self was silent on that point. Maybe it didn't do to dwell on unlikely scenarios. He knew their predicament as well, if not better, than she did as it was *his* job hanging between them. *Because I'm unwilling to do long-distance, even for a short time.*

Am I being unreasonable?

But when he gets back to Nashville, everything will settle back the way it was. He'll jump right back into his job and planning Michael's March. And there's Taylor, whoever they are. After a few months, Ryan will forget all about our island romance. He will...

She leaned back on the pillow, clamping her eyes shut. *Do not cry. Do not cry. DO NOT CRY!*

"Hey," Ryan said, sitting down past her feet.

"Hey." He slipped off one of her espadrilles, then the other. "What are you doing?"

"Are you ticklish?" he asked, pressing his thumb into her right arch and sliding toward the ball of her foot. When he repeated the motion, she moaned. "You like?"

"I like. Don't you dare stop."

Flirting with Ryan felt as natural as breathing. *Enjoy it while it lasts, even if it can't mean anything. I'll survive that, right?*

"I've been thinking."

"That's dangerous." At that, he brushed his thumb under her toes. "Hey! That tickles. Sorry, you were saying?"

"I've been thinking," he repeated, his voice deepening with the pressure of the massage, "that we could invite some food truck chefs over from the mainland. They might be interested in sharing a couple of their recipes with our kitchen crew for compensation and free advertising."

Chapter Twenty-Eight: Claire

He moved on to her heel and ankle. "Couldn't we search online for recipes? That's free."

"There's a difference between following a written recipe and seeing someone cook it in front of you. Our people could learn a lot."

When his hands caressed her lower calf, her intimacy meter shot through the roof. She tugged that foot free and demanded the other one receive the same care and attention.

"Equal treatment," she explained, finding him watching her. A little worm of fear niggled in her gut. "You're good at this. Get a lot of practice?"

"Are you fishing?" he asked, loosening her arch.

"Maybe."

He pressed his thumbs to the ball of her foot, spreading out her toes. *Man, he's good.* It should be noted she was losing the best foot masseuse this side of the Mississippi. *Tough break.*

"If I said yes, would you be jealous?"

She shifted her legs, but he held her foot firmly. "Maybe."

His laugh rumbled through her. "The answer is no. You have pretty feet, by the way. Not all women have pretty feet."

"Are you a foot guy, then?" She poked him in the abs with her big toe. He grabbed her foot with a warning. "Some people have a thing about feet."

"Maybe other people's feet," he said, resting hers on the seat as he rose, "but not yours. There's only one thing wrong with your feet right now." *Oh no...* "They stink!"

She dissolved in a fit of giggles while he excused himself to the head. Between their scrumptious lunch, an incredible kiss, the motion of the boat, the warm sun, and the foot treatment – *phew!* – Claire was plum tuckered out! When he returned, she was fast asleep.

* * *

After a long night of regrets and second-guessing, Claire determined to avoid all physical contact with Ryan. That man was too good. His touch, too exhilarating. He even gave a killer foot massage.

One thing was clear: touching needed to be off limits. Even when the Ryan hesitating in her office doorway looked as good as Cary Grant in *To Catch a Thief*. Come to think of it, personality-wise, he did remind her of her movie crush. *Oh boy.* She was falling for him like Grace Kelly's Frances Stevens.

Thank goodness for solid wood desks! Hers would bolster her emotional barrier.

"Good morning," he said, appearing to litmus test her mood.

"Morning," she replied. "Have a seat and shut the door."

"That might be kind of hard to do in that order, don't you think?" He propped himself against the doorframe as if in a menswear ad, grey slacks and a blue linen button-up to boot. Was it as soft as it looked?

No looking, Claire.

"Shut the door, Ryan." She waved to the chair opposite her desk.

"Yes, ma'am." Once he was seated, he continued. "I feel like I've been called to the principal's office."

"Maybe you should be." *Wait. No flirting, either.* "I like your idea of updating the menus, and I'm on board with the plan we discussed yesterday. Can you take care of that? I wouldn't know where to start."

He stared at her mouth. When she pressed her lips together, he clenched his jaw and looked away.

"I'll look into it."

Forcing herself to relax, she leaned back in her rolling chair, crossed her legs, and tapped her pen on her desk. Totally cool.

"I've been thinking..." She paused automatically, waiting for him to tease her. When he clammed up shut, she cleared her throat. "I would like to hear your other ideas for the park."

When he wasn't forthcoming, she feared what impression she'd given

Chapter Twenty-Eight: Claire

him. Was he afraid she would shoot everything down? *Oops. Maybe he has a point.*

"Please, Ryan."

"I've noticed some things," he replied slowly, "that I believe need our attention."

"Go on."

He appeared to weigh his options for the least offensive one. "First, let's discuss the unused spaces. In real estate, it's good practice to stage properties to give buyers ideas of how the space might be best utilized, as well as to show it in its natural, used state."

"Ryan..."

"Hear me out, Claire, please. This concept applies to public spaces too. Think about a public park. Spaces that appear to have no use tend to be avoided like black holes. Without props, people don't know what to do with them." He shifted, his shoulders filling out...*No. Looking. Claire.* Pen and paper. *Pen and paper.* "Even a bench and a couple of potted plants can give a space a 'lived-in' vibe that looks natural rather than empty. It gives it a purpose, and people like things to have a purpose. It feels 'right.'"

"So, we space the benches out better and move some plants around." She wrote that on her legal pad.

"It's more than that, but that would be a good start."

"Explain."

Chapter Twenty-Nine: Claire

Ryan pulled his chair closer to the desk. "Some parks, amusement and public, have activity centers for kids, outdoor exhibits, or art installations. Stuff like that."

"Art installations? This is an amusement park." She twirled her pen. City living was doing things to Ryan's head.

"I know, but what about activity centers or outdoor exhibits?"

"Maybe on the kids' activities, even though I don't know what those would be, but what do you mean by exhibits? This isn't a museum."

"You've said it yourself, Claire. Pony Island is a historic site. Even though we're a working amusement park, there is amazing history here. Why couldn't we showcase that for everyone to see?" He motioned to the pictures on her walls. "All of these could be scanned and reprinted with captions on weatherproof boards, like at national parks."

"But how much would that cost?"

"We'd start with one or two," he replied, unwilling to back away from his bone of an idea.

"Guess I'll put it on the list of *possibilities*, but I doubt people would come to stand and read about our history."

"No, they wouldn't. That's not the draw. It's part of the backdrop.

Chapter Twenty-Nine: Claire

Things like that add motion to static spaces."

"Wow." She tried not to giggle, and failed. "You sound like an HGTV host."

He laughed. "I guess Taylor's rubbing off on me."

Claire's vision turned green as Ryan absentmindedly rubbed the back of his neck.

"How about those kids' activities?" she asked stiffly. "Are we talking camp games? Electronics?"

"No. Something much simpler. I like the idea of a scavenger hunt where they're searching for fun facts rather than items. Give them a list. They complete it and bring it back for a little prize." He must have seen the same dollar signs because he clarified. "A park-themed sticker or something cheap like that. Kids don't care about the dollar amount."

"But parents do."

"No, parents care about keeping their kids happy and maintaining their sanity. If a five-cent sticker comes between them and a meltdown, they'll take it."

"Touché." She added cheap stickers to the list. "What else?" When he didn't speak up, she sought eye contact. "Don't tell me that's all."

"No…" When she arched her brow, he blew out his breath. "Please don't take this the wrong way, but I've noticed that general park upkeep is…lacking."

Her knuckles turned white around her ink pen. "What do you mean?"

"I'm not talking about cleanliness. It's the chipped and peeling paint, overgrown flowerbeds, and…"

"What?!" *How have I not noticed? Why has no one said anything?*

"Hey, hey, listen, Claire. When we see a place day in, day out, we don't notice things that visitors do. We put off the need, get used to it, and eventually, it feels like it's supposed to be that way." He half rose. "Maybe we need to do a walkthrough. Try to look at the park fresh."

"Wait," she said, motioning him down. "I'll go, but is there anything else you wanted to bring up?"

A white-tailed deer in the headlights would have appeared more with it.

"Uh, well...we need to talk about the rides."

"What's wrong with the rides?" she roared, flinging her hands up. The pen went flying, and Ryan ducked for cover. "Do you want to replace those too?"

"The ones which are broken down."

"What? Are you serious, Ryan?" Fuming, she could barely tolerate his traitorous presence.

"No. Yes. Listen." When he confirmed she wasn't going to kill him with her office supplies, he explained. "The Eye of the Hurricane has been out of order for..."

"Three years."

"Why?"

"The manufacturer went out of business, and we can't get the parts. Modern equivalents won't work on that model."

"So, the ride is going to sit there and..."

"I get your point, but," she willed him to remember a moment he'd clearly forgotten, "the Eye is special."

The Sand Dollar's tinkling melody floated in the open window, blending in harmony with the giggles of the children and the calls of the gulls. The gentle surf brought the depth which made the other sounds pop. Never had Claire visited a place as in tune as Pony Island.

"It is, but we can't hold on to every bit of the past, honey." There he went, melting her with endearments. "Some things have to go...to make room for new memories."

She wanted to cry. *Drat mascara!*

"On top of that," he continued, "leaving broken rides gives guests the unrealistic hope they'll reopen. It's also pretty depressing to look at."

Sulking, she said, "Do you want to kill off Harvey and the Man-of-

Chapter Twenty-Nine: Claire

War too?"

"Can we afford to fix them?"

"Not yet, but the parts are available."

"Then," he replied, "we'll wait on those. Maybe...maybe..." *Maybe what, Ryan?* "You and I could choose a new ride to replace the Eye... together."

"When we can afford it," she said, keeping a straight face. Leave it to Ryan to romance her, not with jewelry, but with an upgrade to their park.

Wait...does this mean he's...

"Let's finish this later," he said, rising. "Whirlpool time?"

"Whirlpool time."

* * *

It's all well and good to set boundaries, but if you do, don't ride a Tilt-A-Whirl together.

"Ryan, you're squishing me!" Claire cried, giggling as she vainly pushed against him. She was 100% confident he was adding his weight to the centrifugal force. She was also 100% confident that in her Ryan-free former life, she hadn't giggled so much – but was that good or bad?

"I can't help it," he replied. Then, the vehicle shifted the opposite direction, sliding them to the other side. "Well, hello there, darling. Come on over."

Her whole side was pressed into his, but thankfully, both of his hands were firmly on the bar next to hers. The familiar tune played as they were knocked and shaken back and forth, back and forth in the jarring seaside waltz.

The clamshell vehicles were specially designed for Pony Island, each painted in pearlescent pink, which Claire now noticed was chipping badly. *Have I become blind to the state of our park?*

When the ride came to a stop, Ryan held up his hand to the ride operator to hold the ride before the next group. The family in line, seeing the state she was in, opted to go elsewhere.

"I can't believe I didn't see it, Ryan," she replied, wiping an escaped tear. "I've failed them."

He reached for her hand, lending his strength. "Who, honey?"

"Our families. My dad, your dad, Gran, Grandpa, Gigi, and Papa. Look at this place. No wonder no one wants to come!"

Ryan pulled her into a hug, stroking her back as she sobbed like a baby. "Sh, Claire. It's not your fault."

"But I should've seen it and addressed it once I became an owner." She sniffed. "Or maybe it wasn't like this…"

Ring, ring! Ryan ignored the call.

"Don't think like that. We can address those issues now. Some of it, we can do ourselves. I'm sure Travis and Kendra will help, as well as our moms and Jack. Maybe even some of the long-time crew – even without overtime."

Ring, ring! Groaning, Ryan checked the screen. *You guessed it – the mysterious Taylor.*

"I'll call back later."

She snuggled into his side, willing him to never let go. Maybe they would die of old age, hugging on the Whirlpool…surrounded by chipped paint.

Ring, ring! "Sorry, Claire. It must be urgent, otherwise…"

"No, it's fine," she replied, easing away and blotting her tears on a used tissue she found in her pocket. "Do I look like a raccoon?"

"The cutest," he said, pausing. He touched her cheek with one hand, his phone in the other. "You sure?"

No. "I should get back to the office, anyway. Make some calls."

"I'll be there as soon as I can," he promised, dialing Taylor as he scooted out of the vehicle. He soon disappeared into the – albeit thin – crowd.

Chapter Thirty: Claire

Someone wanted Ryan back in Nashville. That much was clear. Now whether they were male or female and what they wanted from him, Claire didn't have a clue. But she did have an imagination, and it was going full force. *I mean, what kind of hold does Taylor have on him that he would leave me crying on the Whirlpool?* It must be a pretty big one.

The obvious answer was girlfriend, but she thought she knew Ryan well enough to know he wouldn't cheat on a girl, even with an old crush. It could be someone from work. That didn't rule out an office romance, only a commitment.

Somehow, that didn't make her feel any better.

"It could be a guy," she reminded herself, flopping into her rolling chair. "A friend or coworker. *Taylor* is about as fifty-fifty as you can get."

It's probably a woman.

Shut up, Claire.

A gorgeous, leggy brunette.

Shut up, Claire!

She flipped to a fresh yellow page on her legal pad, her blue ballpoint

Chapter Thirty: Claire

pen poised to write. What did they need to do?
1) **Paint**
2) **Flowerbeds**
3) *He's not here yet.*

"Shut up!"

"I didn't say anything yet," Travis said, his head poking past the door. Claire jumped like she'd been poked with a branding iron.

"Oh my goodness! Travis, forgive me!"

His eyes, too much like Ryan's, searched her office. "Who were you talking to?"

"Myself."

He fiddled with her door knob. "Ah. I've been there. Is this a bad time?"

"That depends. Are you here to tell me what else is wrong with Pony Island?"

"No. Kendra and I need to leave early today. We have a…thing."

It's none of my business. None. Of. My. Business.

"Sure. That's fine."

"Good. Cool. Good luck with," he waggled his fingers, "whatever you're dealing with."

"Thanks." *I'm going to regret this.* "Hey, Trav? Who's Taylor?"

"Taylor?"

"Ryan keeps getting calls from someone named Taylor. I was… wondering." *Shoot.*

"Why don't you ask Ryan?" When she looked down at her hands, he relented. "As far as I know, Taylor is a coworker. I can't tell you anything else."

"Can't or won't."

"Can't. I don't know anything else."

"You're no help."

"Them's the breaks, kid. See you later."

A group photo from when they were in middle school caught her eye. Four kids grinning in front of the Rolling Waves Coaster. *Maybe Ryan and I are caught up in the nostalgia of our past,* she thought, forcing herself back to work. *Am I selfish for wanting him to stay?*

* * *

Clark: I'm sorry, but something's come up with work. Heading to Mom's to deal with it. Can we meet for dinner?

Claire typed out several responses, settling with none at all. Did she want to have dinner with Ryan? *Yes!* She wanted to have all future dinners with Ryan Lanier, but that was impossible. It was time to face that fact.

Breaking for lunch, she skipped her brought-from-home PB&J and headed to visit Miss Hattie. Taking her usual chair in the kitchen, she watched the older woman bustle about, giving orders, and making everyone – from the sous chef to the garbage person – feel valued. What would they ever do without her? Miss Hattie *was* Piper's Restaurant.

"What's wrong, child?" The older woman set a chicken salad croissant sandwich and fries in front of Claire, complete with a heaping cup of fry sauce. Claire wasn't sure she could ever eat fry sauce again…without thinking of Ryan. *You didn't think I meant* ever, *did you? Then, you haven't tasted our fry sauce!*

"Does Pony Island look run-down to you?" Claire blurted, stabbing a grape with her fork. It shot off her plate and rolled to the floor. *Figures.* Miss Hattie observed her for a minute.

"Maybe a little rough around the edges, but nothing that can't be fixed with elbow grease."

"Then, you noticed it too. I was, apparently, oblivious."

"Sometimes, it's hard to see what's right in front of you." Her old friend poured two glasses of sweet tea. "Now, what are you going to

Chapter Thirty: Claire

do about it?"

"How do you always do that?" Claire asked, sniffling.

"Do what?"

"Nothing ever bothers you. You never sulk or give in. You're always ready to tackle a challenge."

Miss Hattie bent back in her chair and cackled. "Goodness, Claire! You think nothing ever bothers me? That I never get riled or upset? That I never feel helpless? Sugar, I'm as human as you."

"But I've never seen you anything but content."

Interlacing her knobby fingers on the table, Miss Hattie leaned forward as if to impart the secret of eternal happiness. Claire mimicked her without a second thought.

"When the good Lord made me," Miss Hattie began, "He made a woman who would lose her first husband in Vietnam and her second after forty years of marriage. He formed a woman who would never have biological children, would work in the same place for over fifty years, and would witness the births and premature deaths of two men she thought of as sons." She laid her worn hands over Claire's. "If I had known all of that when I was twenty, I would've gone crazy. It was time and trust that got me to where I am today."

"I don't think I'll ever be like you, Miss Hattie," Claire replied, wrapping her thumbs around her friend's precious, talented fingers. "You're special."

"As are you, Claire Alice Hensley. Has anyone ever told you, you're like your Gran?"

"I am?"

"When I started working here, I'd never met a woman with more fortitude. Every time we had a setback, Miss Alice would rally the troops and put us to work."

"But that's not me at all!"

"Isn't it? This park was your grandmother's dream." She squeezed

Claire's hands. "If I'm not mistaken, it's yours too."

Claire nodded.

"And you've already stood up to Ryan when he was ready to throw in the towel. If you can stand up to that hunk, don't you think you can do anything you put your mind to?"

"Miss Hattie! Better not let him hear that. It'll go to his head." Leave it to Miss Hattie to bring a little sunshine. When they finished laughing, she continued. "When you put it like that, I guess I need to 'rally the troops,' as you say."

"Yes, ma'am!" Miss Hattie pushed herself up. "Trust in that pretty head of yours, Claire. God put you here for a reason. Maybe it's to save the park, or maybe not, but one thing's for certain. You're the right person for the job."

"Thanks, Miss Hattie, for everything."

As Claire pondered how on Pony Island she could possibly rally her troops, she noticed the purple foxgloves swaying in the restaurant's back garden. Those very flowers were the ones her dad gave her mom for their first anniversary, starting their yearly tradition. How had Claire forgotten that? Would it hurt her mother to see their special flower on her and Jack's wedding day? If Jack found out, would he be upset too?

"Oh no...I've ruined Mom and Jack's wedding!"

And it was too late to order new flowers.

Chapter Thirty-One: Ryan

"My father is impressed with how you closed the deal with the Lioness," Taylor said, her warm voice matching her smile on the video call. Ryan shook his head with a laugh, catching sight of the old Carolina Panthers poster on his bedroom wall.

"I don't feel like I did anything other than give her an ultimatum of sorts. Do they really call Ms. Ross the Lioness?"

"For good reason. She not only dresses, uh…" She adjusted her earbuds, her cheeks turning pink. Ryan pinched the bridge of his nose, clamping his eyes shut.

"Let's not go there."

Taylor grimaced. "No, let's not. She's one of the city's fiercest agents. She knows how to get what her clients want, but somehow, she talked them into that loft space. All. Because. Of. You."

"I'm glad it's over."

"You know she'll request you again, though."

Taylor disappeared to hand someone a file, taking her cheerful presence with her. Ryan checked his notifications again, but Claire hadn't responded. His leg jiggled as he rubbed his sweaty palms together. A simple text, *Yes* or *No*, was all he needed. The not knowing, that was the killer.

"Be pre-PARED!" Taylor sang upon her return.

"You did not."

"I did." She pointed to the camera. "And guess what? I've heard rumors of a potential promotion for *someone*."

"Me?"

"Yes, you!" She sipped her coffee, trying to look innocent. "The proof should hit your inbox soon."

"What?"

"The Big Three are considering three agents for one slot, but you're looking good. The thing is, they want you back here ASAP to prove you're serious about your job." Taylor bent forward. "What's your ETA?"

His old desk chair, the one in which he'd spent more time dreaming about Claire than studying, creaked under his adult weight. "I'm not sure. Selling is off the table for now. We need more time to figure this out."

"Don't take too long," Taylor replied, pursing her lips. "You're missed. Plus, Tri-Star's backing out really threw Dom for a loop. He's a great guy, but he's not good with change, believe me."

"I know. I'll text as soon as I know something…on both accounts."

Sure enough, an email from the bosses sat in his inbox informing him he was up for promotion. They wanted to know when he was coming back. He responded with his thanks and as vague of an update as possible. He didn't feel right airing the park's dirty laundry outside of the company.

The call with Taylor was longer than he anticipated – two hours longer – and hadn't been as urgent as he feared. Even though he texted, Claire had every right to be upset with him, if she was. He left her crying to deal with work stuff. *What a jerk! How can I make this up to her?*

Chapter Thirty-One: Ryan

Chocolate? Flowers? Dinner? A movie? *No, no, no, no!* Too cliché, too trite, too lame.

How does a man in love apologize?

A man *in love?*

Lightheaded, he braced himself on the wall of the upstairs hallway. *Am I in love with Claire?* The very idea sent a shock wave through his system. The confirmation was staring him in the face, literally.

A photo hung right in front of him of the four kids in high school: Travis, Kendra, Claire, and Ryan. Travis had his arm slung around Kendra's shoulders, pulling her close. One of Claire's arms was wrapped around her best friend's waist as she and the others grinned at the camera. Her other arm was reaching behind him, and he remembered the moment as if it was yesterday.

"C'mon, Ryan! Get in the photo," Travis said. "We have to preserve this moment forever."

"Yay!" Kendra added. "Junior and senior years, here we come!"

Claire smiled shyly, waving him over. "The picture's not complete without you, Ryan."

How did I miss that?

Racing down the stairs, he rounded into the living area and stopped cold. His mom sat crumpled on the sofa crying, a photo of his dad gripped in her hand. All other thoughts fled as he jogged to her side.

"Mom, what's wrong?"

Helene dabbed her tears. "Ryan! I didn't know you were here." *Sniff.* "Another tidal wave hit. I miss him so much."

"I do too, Mom." He pulled her into a hug, remembering how she used to be the one hugging him.

"I know you do, baby." She laid the photo on the coffee table. "This house is full of memories. Everywhere I turn, I see something that reminds me of your father. I keep expecting him to come around the corner or to hear him moving about. Natalie's been getting me out of the house, but with her engagement to Jack..."

"*Sh*, Mom," he said, rubbing her back. "I understand."

"Sometimes, I think it would be easier to start fresh somewhere else rather than be surrounded by all these memories." She straightened. "Perhaps moving to Nashville with you would be a good change. Spend some time with my other son."

Ryan's mouth went dry. *Mom is thinking of moving to Nashville?* If living on the island was painful, a change of scenery might be what she needed. How could he deny her – the woman who'd given him a lifetime of love and care?

"Think about it, and we'll talk later," he heard himself say. "I would love to have you nearby. I've missed you, Mom."

"You too, sweetie. I won't hold you up any longer." She patted his leg. "I'll be fine in a moment. You run along."

* * *

"Ooo, I like that one," Claire said as she leaned over Morgan's shoulder. Jacob sat at the computer next to them, his face scrunched in concentration.

Finally a light pink, Claire's hair was pulled back in a clip, a few strays brushing her cheek. Her beautiful face was free of makeup, her smile, natural in color. As long as he lived, Ryan would never forget that kiss.

He paused out of sight to observe her, sealing up the memory. He would need it on the long drive home and for months afterward.

The hope birthed upon seeing the old photo faded with his mom's predicament. As the oldest son, it was time for him to step up and take his father's place. If his mom wanted to leave the island, he didn't want her to go alone...and he wouldn't drag Claire into it. As they weren't in a relationship – and weren't likely to be any time soon – he didn't feel right sharing his mother's private thoughts without her permission.

Chapter Thirty-One: Ryan

It's time to let go.

"What are y'all up to?" Ryan asked, walking to the other side of Jacob.

"Yikes, man!" the boy said, jumping as if Ryan was a rattler. "Sneaking up on people? Not cool."

"Ja-cob," Morgan said. "Hi, Mr. Lanier! Claire asked us to update the website."

"Call me Ryan, please. You're making me feel old." Morgan acquiesced, a pretty bloom darkening her freckles. When Jacob's fingers froze over the keyboard, Ryan cringed inside. *Time for a redirect.* "Hey, buddy, looks like you're coding?"

"Yes, sir." Jacob's tight response dissolved into an animated explanation Ryan didn't understand. When he took a tiny breath, Claire jumped in.

"Thanks, Jacob. You're doing great!" She sought Ryan's attention, but he pretended to be absorbed in Morgan's screen.

"Social media? What's the plan here?"

Morgan, appearing to sense the tense atmosphere, deferred to Claire.

"I gave in to this girl's pleas. She's setting me up on social media, and she's going to help me, right?"

"Yes. Her username is PIAPVintageGirl, if you want to follow her. We're going to take photos of Claire's clothes every day, along with the old-fashioned things she does, and tell others how they can do the same stuff if they want. Part fun, part educational. It'll be good advertisement for the park too!"

Claire wrapped her arms around her waist, mimicking the style of her blue floral dress. "I doubt it will take off, but it's worth a try."

"You might be surprised," Ryan said, searching for encouragement. "My friend Taylor has a fashion account, hair and makeup too, with over 20,000 followers. She says people eat that stuff up."

He pulled up FashvilleChick615 and scrolled to Taylor's feed. He smiled at one shot of typically modern Taylor trying a vintage hairstyle that reminded him of Claire.

"See? You'll be in good company. I'll send her your username."

Swallowing visibly, Claire laser-beamed in on Morgan's computer. "She's pretty."

Ryan blinked. "She is." *But she's got nothing on you,* he wanted to add, but it wasn't the time or place. A rock settled in his stomach. *And it never will be.*

"We've got this if y'all have other things to do," Morgan said.

"Which means," Claire replied, patting her on the shoulder, "we're distracting you. We'll get out of your hair."

He followed Claire to her office and closed the door. "Sorry I took so long. Work stuff – you know how that goes – but I'm, uh, up for promotion."

"Oh." Then, she came back to port. "That's great, Ryan! Wonderful! Super! I'm sure you deserve it."

He rubbed the back of his neck. "It's not been decided, but Taylor says her father's impressed with my work. She thinks I have a good shot."

"I'm sure you do." She lowered herself into her chair, and he followed suit. "When will you know?"

"A week or two, but they, uh, she asked when I'm coming home. I wasn't sure what to tell her."

"Then, it sounds like we need to make some decisions." Reaching for a pen, she sat poised to write. "Are you willing to give me until next season to turn things around?"

"Yes."

"I'll make sure we stay on track with what we've already discussed, and we'll keep in touch via email and text. Oh, and it would probably be good for us to meet with Mr. Dunlap once more before you leave."

"Probably." He watched her pen while she scribbled notes, but his mind was numb.

Chapter Thirty-One: Ryan

"Morgan's starting us a blog too. Do you think people would enjoy seeing 'before-and-afters' and stuff like that? Show how we're updating the park?"

"Probably."

She added that to her list. "I think that's it, then." She missed as she capped her pen, marking her finger in blue. "Do you plan to stay for Mom and Jack's wedding this weekend?"

"Yeah. I can leave on Monday, I guess. That will work."

"There you go. It sounds like a plan." Claire noticed the pen mark, licked the thumb of her other hand, and started scrubbing. "There's the cake tasting tomorrow, if you want to come." Not satisfied, she tried another lick.

Don't make this harder on yourself, Ryan! Say no.

"How can I say no to free cake?" he replied, his heart breaking.

"Who said it was free?" *I can't take your flirting, Claire. It's killing me.* She sensed his telepathic plea and went back to her thumb when her phone dinged. "I have a new follower. FashvilleChick615. Taylor?"

"Yeah. It's a combination of 'fashion' and 'Nashville,' along with the area code."

"I gathered that. I see you follow her." She sent him a follow request. He returned it with fear in his chest. *Will I be able to see her gorgeous face in my feed without dying a little each time?*

"As a friend," he replied. "Her content isn't exactly my type."

"No, I suppose not." She scrolled down what he assumed was Taylor's feed. "She's *very* pretty, Ryan."

She's fishing. When he didn't respond immediately, her thumb froze. *Should I tell her?* It was a long time ago, but in the interest of honesty, he would.

"We went on a couple dates when I started at the firm, but we decided we're better off friends." He shifted, unsticking his arm from the chair's varnish. "She ended up marrying Dominic, and now, they have two kids."

"Oh."

"Obviously, there's nothing going on. We're good friends."

When a call came over her walkie-talkie app, he knew their time was up. Rising together, they paused before opening the door. Her upturned face held a world of hurt.

"Work, friends, or not, you've left me every time she calls." *Even when I was crying,* he knew. "I think it's clear where you belong."

You don't know the other half of it. He stared down into her red-rimmed eyes. *It's out of my control. I'm trapped.*

"I need to go do *my* job now," she said. "Guess I'll see you later?"

He nodded, unable to speak. As they parted ways, he vowed in his heart to do everything he could to save the park…to make up for leaving her all over again.

Chapter Thirty-Two: Claire

Claire: The Dolphin Dive has officially sprung a leak. *spiral eyes*
Clark: How bad?
Claire: Nothing major. A few days, they said.
Clark: That's good.

She hovered over the edit option. Should she change his name in her contacts to 'Ryan'? *Would that make this easier?*

"After he leaves."

Claire entered the office to find Jacob and Morgan wrapping things up. The boy was much more at ease than earlier in the day. Somehow or other, the two worked through the awkwardness. Claire silently wished them the best.

"Miss Claire," Jacob said, "what do you think?"

As he navigated their updated website, Claire marveled at how much he'd accomplished. A fresh color scheme of sky blue, navy, white, and black was accented with pops of red and yellow, bringing to mind summers with friends, hot dogs with ketchup and mustard, *and a certain boy who shall not be named.*

"I love it! I'm impressed, Jacob." He beamed with the praise. "I should've asked you to do this sooner."

"Morgan's got you all set up on social media with a matching color scheme. We used the same hex codes and everything."

"I have no idea what you said, but it all looks amazing. Thank y'all so much!"

Morgan offered a hug, warming Claire's heart. Jacob swamped them all in a bear hug. Maybe Miss Hattie was right. *This is where I'm meant to be.*

"We're going to get ice cream," Morgan said. "Wanna come?"

Claire bit back a giggle at Jacob's expression. "No, but thank you. You two have fun."

As the boy grinned his relief, they set out for what might become a first date. Time would tell.

Claire met Ryan at the Carou-Sail an hour later to squeeze in a quick ride before meeting with Mr. Dunlap. As she mounted one of her favorite horses, a white charger with a coral-pink scalloped saddle and scaled legs, she felt an unfamiliar peace settle over her.

No matter what ultimately happens with the park, things are moving forward. We have a plan, and we're going to give it our best effort. If it fails, at least we'll go out fighting.

She and Ryan had come to terms with their past...and their future. *No matter our feelings, our lives aren't meant to be lived together.* Maybe there was someone else out there for her, or maybe not. Either way, she was determined to be content.

They spoke little as the carousel circled round and round, the calliope crooning its own version of Bing Crosby's 'The Anniversary Waltz.' Once they could afford it, Claire wanted to bring in a specialist to restore it. She prayed it would last until then. They didn't need another ride breaking down.

"I love this time of the day," she said, resting her temple on the golden post. "Once the park closes, it's like we're draped in a magic spell until

Chapter Thirty-Two: Claire

daybreak."

"I've never thought of it that way," Ryan said, looking everywhere but at her. "Once I started working here, I was glad the day was done."

"You always wanted out, didn't you?"

He weighed his words. "I did. This island was tiny compared with the rest of the world. I've been fortunate to travel many places, mostly in the States. It's a beautiful world out there."

"Do you ever miss this?" she asked as the ride came to a stop. They hopped off before he spoke, his face turned toward the sunset.

"We should head out. The lawyer's office closes at six."

She didn't press him, preferring to enjoy what time they had left to parting mad.

Mr. Dunlap was pleased with their progress and promised to report to the Pony Island Corporation. A little after six, they left the office, lingering in each other's presence.

"We could grab dinner," she suggested, hope threatening to choke her. "Eat in the tower."

"No, I better get back to Mom. She's having a hard time."

"Oh! Obviously, you should spend time with her. I'm sorry." She rubbed her upper arms even though it wasn't chilly. "Will I see you at the tasting?"

"Wouldn't miss it."

* * *

The next morning dawned dark and rainy, and Claire overslept. She skipped her hair and makeup, shoving her hair up into a snood. The somber black bow fit her mood perfectly. She was sipping a cup of strong coffee and staring out at the swelling ocean when a text pinged in.

Natalie: Woke up with a head cold. Can I trust you to choose a cake?

Claire: Oh no! Of course. Can I bring you anything?

Natalie: No. Jack dropped by on his way to work. Something came up, and he won't be able to make it either.

If she didn't know better, she would think this had 'scheme' written all over it – but she hadn't confided in her mom about her feelings for Ryan.

Claire: OK. I'll text you later.

Outside, dressed in her slicker and rain boots, she opted for her golf cart. It wasn't much protection, but it would be better than her bike. By the time she arrived at the Beachcomber's back entrance, she was chilled to the bone.

Ryan sat in the private dining room, a forgotten mug of coffee warming his hands. He roused as she removed her wet things and put on a pair of tennies.

"Morning," he said. Taking a sip, he grimaced. "Cold."

"I'll ask for two more," she replied, "and let them know we're ready. Mom and Jack can't make it."

Fifteen minutes of painful small talk later, they sat side by side with six wedding cake flavors spread out before them. Determined to keep things light, Claire read the labels out loud.

"'Key Lime to My Heart,' 'Red Velvet Rose,' 'Praline to a Kiss' – Oh! That's a spin on 'Prelude to a Kiss,' right? – 'I Love You a Chocolatté,' 'In Vain-illa I Have Struggled' – Ha! *Pride and Prejudice.* Nice! – and 'Twenty-Four Carrot.' They all look yummy. Where should we start?"

"Chocolate?" He reached for a sample, and she slapped his hand away.

"No! That's too obvious. We need a strategy."

"For a cake tasting?"

She surveyed the choices. "We need to make sure we're getting the full flavor of each one, so we can make an informed decision."

He rested his elbows on the table, warming a little. "How about we

Chapter Thirty-Two: Claire

go in strength of flavor? Save the 'obvious' for last?"

"I like that. Vanilla, then?"

As soon as Claire tasted Mr. Darcy's cake, she realized their plan already failed. This was the best vanilla cake ever. *As it should be.*

"Oh, that's good," Ryan said with a moan. "I wasn't expecting that."

"It's the Madagascar vanilla," the baker explained. "We also add a touch of almond to the icing."

"It's lovely," Claire agreed. "What now? I'm thinking red velvet."

"Isn't that basically chocolate with a boatload of red food coloring?" Ryan asked.

"Pretty much, but it's a familiar flavor. The others look like they have an extra kick."

Wrong again! The richness exploded with the perfect amount of sweetness. And the cream cheese icing? *To die for!*

"Are you all right over there?" Ryan asked, amused.

"We're in over our heads," she stage-whispered. "Maybe we need one of each."

"That can be arranged," the baker replied with a snicker, "but I don't think it's what your mother had in mind."

"Definitely not."

Carrot was next, but as tasty as it was, it reminded Claire too much of her father. "Carrot was Dad's favorite. We'd better steer clear of that one."

"Understood," the baker replied, removing it from the table.

The lime, boasting the same silky frosting as the red velvet, was dismissed for not being a Key lime pie instead, leaving the praline and chocolate. As soon as Claire set the praline cake on her tongue, she wondered how anything could beat it.

"Oh, that's amazing! You have to try this, Ryan." He froze, staring at her offering as he might a shark. *Our kiss started like this.* As if it was a prickly sea urchin, she dropped it back on the plate. "Sorry. Here, let me get you a new…"

"No! It's fine," he said, inhaling it. She wasn't convinced he even tasted it. "It's good."

One to go. The chocolate was as luscious as predicted, that hint of espresso sending it over the top. Claire pointed, her other hand covering her mouth.

"Mmm-hmm."

"'I Love You,'" Ryan began, catching Claire mid-chew. His Adam's apple bobbed as he finished with, "'a Chocolatté,' then?"

I love you too, Ryan. "It's the 'obvious' choice."

"Obviously."

Chapter Thirty-Three: Claire

They prepared to leave as the baker boxed up the rest of the samples for them to take home.

"It's raining cats and dogs out there," Ryan said, peering into the gloom. "What's your plan?"

"Make a break for my golf cart, I guess," she replied, switching her tennies for boots. Her raincoat was still wet. *That's going to be fun.*

"Here, let me help." Ryan held out her coat, keeping the wet side away from her dry clothes. Instead of the chill she expected, warmth enveloped her like a hug.

"Thank you."

"You're welcome," he replied by her ear. He didn't touch her, but the husky timbre of his voice stirred the embers best left to cool. Gently, he poked her hair covering. "What's this thing? It's like a hairnet, but thicker."

"A snood. How does it look?"

When he paused, she wasn't sure if he was examining it or weighing his answer. She glanced over her shoulder to catch his longing before it shuttered closed.

"It's cute. You should have Morgan take a picture and post it."

Before she could protest with the facts – she threw it on, wasn't wearing makeup, and considered the weather, not a photoshoot, when she picked out her clothes – Ryan pulled out his phone. His deep inhale shuddered through him.

"One for me?"

"You sure you want that?" she replied. *To remind you of what can never be.*

"Please?"

"If you get in it with me and send me a copy."

He positioned himself slightly behind her and turned the camera to selfie mode. "Ready?"

She smiled sadly at Ryan's handsome face rather than the camera lens. One click, and it was done. He eased back, tapping for a moment. Her cell dinged with a message from 'Clark.'

"Are you going to change that?" he asked.

"Not yet." She saved the photo. "What's your plan for the day?"

"Travis asked for my help. I'd better get to their house."

"Then, I guess I'll see you at the wedding?"

"Wouldn't miss it," he replied, not moving. *We're stalling.* There was one thing to do: rip off the Band-Aid. She tied the belt on her slicker and gave a little wave, backing away.

"Goodbye, Ry-AH!"

Her rubber heel slipped on the slick tile. Arms flailing, she braced for the crash. Faster than a speeding bullet, Ryan swooped in and saved her from potential harm and certain embarrassment.

"Whoa there," he said, cradling her as picture-perfect as a movie scene, the kiss potential mere inches away. "Are you okay?"

"I think so," she replied, her hands resting on his strong shoulders. How tempted she was to encircle his neck and gift him with a hearty thank you! Instead, she made her way to her feet with his help. Soon, she was standing Ryan-free and lonely. "Thank you. I'll be more careful from now on."

She left, fearing another moment in his presence would break her. But in the time it took to putt to work in the deluge, shake off her rain gear, and fix a strong cup of hot tea, she knew it was hopeless.

I will always be in love with Ryan Lanier.

Before she could stop herself, she sent him a text.

Claire: You owe me a ride on the Widow's Walk. 6:00?

She wrapped her hands around her warm mug as she waited. One minute passed. Two minutes. Three.

Clark: I'll be there this time. I promise.

And when he was, she would tell him exactly how she felt. Maybe this time, it would sway his plans.

* * *

"Have you checked social media this morning?" Morgan asked, giddily tapping her fingertips together.

"No…" Claire replied, looking between the girl and Jacob.

"You already have…" Morgan said as Jacob provided the drumroll, "300 followers! Eep!"

Claire pulled up her account and pointed to the number. "357. That's, um, good, right?"

"That's amazing!" Jacob clarified, holding out his fist for a fist bump. She gave him one, reeling. *357 people want to see what clothes I put on every day or learn the ways of the past?*

"Is this normal?"

"No!" Morgan cried. "And I've been filtering out the spam accounts and creepy men. Most, if not all, of those people are real! And you have Ryan's friend Taylor to thank for a bunch of it. She shared your account in her posts."

Taylor, huh? And to think I was jealous of the woman. Oops.

"What do we do now?" Claire asked, her mind in a fog.

Morgan swept her hair over her shoulder. "I think we need a celebratory photoshoot. You look adorable – elegant meets practical."

"I look like something that crawled out of the ocean," Claire replied, tucking a stray lock back into her snood. "Have you been outside this morning?"

"You don't look that bad, Miss Claire," Jacob said, earning a frown from Morgan. "Sorry."

"Ignore him. You're as pretty as a mermaid."

Resigned, Claire followed Morgan's instructions, posing in front of her closet door. Jacob chimed in with advice, and despite his help, Morgan was satisfied in about fifteen minutes. *How many shots did she take?* Claire hadn't a clue but guessed it numbered in the mid-fifties.

"One more, Claire," Morgan said, coming in close. "Now, think of the one thing you want most in life." *Click!* "Great! I'll sort through these and get them uploaded."

Claire thanked them and fell into her chair with a *whoosh!* Was this going to be her every morning from now on? *I hope not!*

As they were leaving, she heard Jacob say, "400, Morgan! We should celebrate!"

"Maybe the Beachcomber for lunch?"

"Uh…yeah! Let's do it…"

The door closed, cutting off their adorably awkward date planning. Claire knew it wasn't her unique style alone that would attract followers; it was Morgan's keen eye and talent. That girl was turning out to be an asset, and Claire would be remiss if she didn't foster her ambitions. Maybe after college, Morgan would return to the park for her career. Jacob too. They needed a good tech guy.

If we're open, she reminded herself, getting to work.

* * *

Chapter Thirty-Three: Claire

"Have you seen Kendra?" Claire asked Jack at lunchtime, pulling her ham and cheese from the office refrigerator.

"She's out today." He punched the start button on the microwave. The familiar smell of her mom's 'Scarborough Fair' pork roast wafted Claire's way. Parsley, sage, rosemary, and thyme. *Home.* "I didn't pry."

Back at her desk, Claire sent her friend a text.

Claire: Everything okay?

After a few tense bites, she responded.

Kendra: I have some things I need to do.

Claire: Can I help?

Kendra: Four gallons of vinegar?

Claire: Sure

Wait. That's a lot of vinegar.

Claire borrowed an umbrella from the crew cast-offs and hurried to the market. Only at the checkout did she realize she couldn't carry four gallons of vinegar and an umbrella. She was going to get soaked! *Where's Prince Charming when you need him?*

No dashing stranger appeared, so she arrived at Kendra's house sopping wet. Inside, she found her friend on her hands and knees cleaning baseboards.

"Oh, good! You brought the vinegar. How much do I owe you?"

"Nothing, but what on earth are you doing?"

Kendra pushed an errant curl off her forehead and went back to scrubbing. "Have you ever realized how dirty baseboards are?"

"No..." That's when Claire noticed the list. Every square inch of the house was noted. Some items were checked off, but more than half were undone. "What's going on? Do you want some help?"

"No! I mean, I've got it. Travis is helping too, now that he and Ryan are finished. Thanks again!"

"If you're sure..."

"Yep!"

Claire paused in the doorway, her chipped red nails gripping the frame. "Are you moving?"

Kendra's hand shot out, but she caught herself before hitting the floor. "No, we're not moving. Why would you think…" She motioned to the baseboard. "Oh…no, it's nothing like that."

Claire waited, but her friend sealed up tight. No answers materialized as she headed back to the office, hoping she had a change of clothes in the closet. If not, she would have to 'make do'…and smell like a wet dog.

Now, that's romantic.

Chapter Thirty-Four: Ryan

"Sure you don't need more help, Trav?" Ryan asked after helping his brother move furniture from room to room and floor to floor. Did his sister-in-law have the redecorating bug? "Kendra's going to town, isn't she?"

"No," Travis replied, hurrying Ryan to the foyer, "we've got it. Thanks, Bro!"

With that, his little brother shut the door in his face. Ryan flipped up the hood of his windbreaker. *The storm outside is nothing compared to the one in that house, that's for sure.* Not wanting to head home, and not ready to run into Claire, he decided to peruse the shops for gifts for friends in Nashville.

The swelling waves of the Atlantic side crashed onto the beach beyond the sand dunes, the brisk wind buffeting his body and whistling through the seams of his clothing. His heart answered the siren's call, part cleansing, part peace. Something to treasure. Nothing in Tennessee filled the chamber long claimed by the sea, and yet, he hadn't missed it for ten years. Why would he now?

It would only remind him of her. *No, it's always reminded me of her.*

Ding! A new post from PlAPVintageGirl. His thumb hovered over the notification. *Am I ready for this?*

He shoved the device into his pocket. Inside the sundry store, he focused on choosing a magnet for Dominic and Taylor, but the itch to check Claire's post wouldn't subside. Hiding behind a t-shirt display, he opened the app.

A pair of eyes the color of the August sea pinned him in place, alight with amusement. He paid no heed to her clothes or hair. It was *Claire* who captivated him. He devoured five photos, freezing on the last one.

As if she was watching through the screen, she sought him and no one else. He knew without a doubt that look, filled with longing and heartbreak, was meant for him. Tearing away, he scrolled down to the description. The last line before the gob of hashtags caught his eye.

'What is the one thing you want most in life? Share your answer below.'

You, Claire. Always you.

I have to make this right.

* * *

"Ryan?" his mom called as he paused in the mudroom to peel off his wet things. "What are you doing here? I thought you were meeting Claire."

She had her Bible study materials spread out on the kitchen table. He hated to bother her, but this was an emergency.

"Mom, are you still thinking about moving to Nashville?"

"Oh, I hadn't thought any more about it. I'm sorry, baby, I got your hopes up." She motioned to their home. "I'm not sure I could leave, at least not for a long while."

"You're sure?"

"Yes…why?"

He kissed her soundly on the cheek. "Thank you, Mom. I love you!"

Chapter Thirty-Four: Ryan

"I love you too, but what on Pony Island…?" A light dawned. "How was the cake tasting? Natalie said she and Jack had to drop out." The twinkle which appeared made him mighty suspicious…and grateful.

"Chocolate," he replied, keeping his hopes to himself. "Although, praline came in a close second."

"I see." She patted his face. "Go get her, sweetie, and don't you dare run away this time."

Taking the stairs two at a time, Ryan raced to his room to change and plan, rifling through his clothes for his grey suit – the one that set those baby blues on fire. He tamed his hair with a little gel, but not *too* much, mussing it for that roguish hero vibe. Tonight, he wanted to look good…*old Hollywood good*…for Claire.

Move over Jimmy Stewart. This girl's mine.

At 5:30, he checked her message one last time.

Kryptonite: You owe me a ride on the Widow's Walk. 6:00?

"I'll be there this time, honey. I promise."

* * *

By 5:45, the rain let up, the sun bathing the island in a golden goodbye. Ryan took the full rainbow, in all its fractured jewels, as a good omen. To ensure he was on time, he arrived early and stood outside the haunted house like a nervous senior.

6:01. *Where is she?*

6:03. Claire stepped into view, her platinum blonde hair washed free of the red dye and loosely curled over her shoulders. Her dress, a rose-pink polka dot number, hugged her curves while giving the illusion of innocence. He held out the bouquet of pink dahlias. *Perfect.*

"You came," she said, cradling the flowers. "How lovely."

"Not as lovely as you, Claire."

"Thank you."

Good. The words got out.

"I like that suit," she concluded after a perusal of her own.

"I noticed." She bloomed as rosy as her dress. He held out his arm, savoring her inability to resist admiring the fruits of his exercise routine. "Shall we? They're waiting for us to close the queue."

In the single-file line, he reached for her hand, leading her at a walk when he wanted to break into a run. Neither spoke, enjoying the other's presence.

An old fiberglass boat waited by the creaky dock, rocking in the current generated by hidden pumps. Ryan boarded before assisting Claire, settling side by side. The robotic crow with red eyes, dubbed 'Evermore,' cawed the familiar warning, and the boat set off into the dim.

"I've only ridden the Widow's Walk a couple of times since high school," Claire said, her hand shaking in his, "to check it. I've never been able to enjoy it again, thinking of…I'm sorry."

"No, Claire," he replied, smoothing his thumb over the back of her hand until she calmed. "I'm the one who's sorry. I should've come, but," he swallowed, "I was afraid you wouldn't be waiting. Your friend Lauren said you liked Kyle, that you wanted me to tell him. I feel stupid now, but I believed her after seeing you laughing with him."

"Kyle? Kyle Merritt? You're joking!"

"No, unfortunately. I was mortified that I sent you that note. For teenaged me, it was easier to avoid you all together than ask you myself."

"It's in the past," Claire said as they floated through the graveyard. Ghosts moaned and tombstones rattled, but Ryan missed all of it.

Should I put my arm around her? No more indecision. She nestled into his side, resting her head on his shoulder. When she spoke, her breath tickled his neck.

"If I don't say this now, I'll burst. I know you have obligations in Nashville, and I admire your dedication, but I don't want to lose you

Chapter Thirty-Four: Ryan

again, Ryan. If we need to do long-distance until we figure things out, I'll do it."

When her mouth brushed the bare skin below his beard, he like to fell out of the boat! *Oh, the temptation...but we're almost there. Don't give in yet, buddy!*

"I'm not going anywhere, honey," he reassured her, "at least not for long." He turned his head away, expecting she would forgive him later. She gave a little whine as their stop came into view. Grabbing her hand, he helped her onto the ledge in front of the haunted house as their boat floated on by. "Come on."

"Where are we going in such a hurry?" she asked, intrigued. He pulled her through the iron gates and past the undead animatronics, his anticipation in high gear. *She's not wearing lipstick!*

Behind the house façade, the nook was exactly as he remembered: the location of his top teenage fantasy – *not that I'll be going about things the same way now.* Tugging her in front of him, he nestled her in, leaving a foot between them in the darkness.

"I've waited fifteen years for this moment," he whispered, drinking her in. The ultraviolet lights made the polka dots on her dress glow like stars, showing the way. "I noticed this nook when I was cleaning one day, and my imagination took off. I couldn't miss the chance to get you back here now."

She slid her hands up his arms, hooking them around his neck. "Are we indulging in teen fantasies now? Mine was getting stuck at the top of the Sand Dollar."

"That can be arranged." He slipped his hold to the small of her back, fingering the soft material, the woman he loved underneath. "Man, I had it bad. I was going to ask you out. Whether I would've had the nerve to bring you here, I don't know," he laughed softly, "and that's probably for the best – but I was determined to spend the summer as your boyfriend."

"I wish you had asked me out," she replied, her fingertips straying to the hair above his collar. The space between them evaporated. "But if you hadn't left early, you would've seen Kyle and I weren't together."

"Maybe things happened this way for a reason," he said, nuzzling her nose. "I needed to get away for a while, and being apart allowed you to find yourself too."

"What now, Ryan Lanier?" The *purr* in her 'r's threw him overboard. "We move forward, Claire Hensley – together."

Chapter Thirty-Five: Claire

Together.

What a beautiful word.

This time, Ryan didn't hesitate, settling Claire into the nook as he might a marble statue. The circle of his embrace was a safe harbor amidst the current surging between them. His scent – the ocean with a heady hint of dark chocolate – mingled with the aroma of forever. Their kisses ebbed and flowed, washing away the longing of the past ten years.

Ryan is mine.

"Tell me this isn't a dream," he whispered, touching her forehead with his.

"It's real, Superman. Everything we've ever wanted."

"But I want so much more, honey." He trailed kisses to her ear, each a footprint in the sand – gone too soon but cherished. "Every day, every hour, every minute of you. I don't want to waste another moment."

His assurances were sunrises on the ocean, his promises, the innumerable stars over the sea.

"'While I breathe, I hope,'" she replied, his short beard tickling her cheek. "I've prayed for this, Ryan, that you would come back to me."

"I'm home now. I know my place is here – with the park, my family, and you." He punctuated each with a kiss, returning to where he started. *I'm floating on cloud nine over the Ecsta-Sea.* As she grinned, giddy, at the pun, he pulled back a smidge. "Love doesn't leave, and I'm not either…except to get my things and deal with work. Will you come with me? I'll show you all Music City has to offer."

"All I want is you, Ryan," she replied, "now and forever. And you're right – the park can get by a few weeks a year without me."

"Honeymoon road trip, then?" he teased. She shoved him back with a jolt.

"Are you asking?"

When Ryan fell to one knee and pulled a box out of his pocket, she like to fainted. He clasped her hand between his, sliding a twisting sterling silver ring with a heart-shaped amethyst onto her ring finger, stopping shy of her second joint.

"This may seem sudden, Claire, but I've loved you since we were kids. I bought this for you before graduation, and it's not a proper engagement ring, but please accept it as my promise. When we're ready, I'll be by your side."

"Oh, Ryan, it's perfect!"

"No, *we're* perfect," he said, wiggling the ring into place. "Two halves of a whole…complete."

"It fits!"

"Good. I think it was a little big when I bought it," he replied, his relief escaping in a chuckle. "Don't take that the wrong way, honey. I like that you're more of a *woman* now." The way he said *woman* erased any possibility of insult.

"I'm not the only one who aged well," she replied, wrapping her arms around his fit waist. "I love you, handsome."

"And I love you, gorgeous." He returned the gesture, danger swirling in those hazel eyes. "Shall we seal the promise, then?"

Chapter Thirty-Five: Claire

They sealed their engagement with a kiss so *full* of promise, she was sure their wedding date wouldn't be too far off. As their resolve slipped down her neck, an extra loud moan let loose...from one of the animatronic ghouls.

"That wasn't me!" Claire blurted, jumping out of his arms with a nervous titter. Ryan, at first full of fire, broke into a howling guffaw loud enough to wake the dead. Claire joined him. They clasped hands as they emerged from their hiding place.

"They're probably wondering where we are, the boat arriving with only a bouquet of dahlias and all," he said.

"No, I doubt that," she said, pointing to the ceiling. A red light blinked back.

"You're joking!" Ryan replied. "I know for a fact that wasn't there ten years ago. I checked."

"We installed them a while back when someone snuck off a boat," she tugged on his lapel, "but not for the same reason."

"Why didn't you say something?"

"And ruin the moment?" She smirked, finding herself back in his arms in front of the oversized gargoyle. "I don't care who sees me kissing you, Ryan Lanier," she nodded at the statue, "even George."

"Well then, George," he replied, lowering his head, "care for an encore?"

With that, the lights and sound in the ride went out, and the intercom came on. "We're out of popcorn over here, so we're going home. Good night, lovebirds!"

"Miss Hattie?!"

* * *

"It's about time you two got together," Travis said, high-fiving Ryan. Claire's fiancé – *eep!* – glanced at her sheepishly.

"We're hearing that a lot this morning."

Family and crew flooded into the conference room for the park meeting. While everyone was excited about their engagement, concern for the park ran rampant. Kendra hooked her arm around Claire's waist.

"Is Ryan as good a kisser as you used to imagine?"

"Gross!" her husband said as Ryan's face turned light tower red. Claire, even though she was sure she matched, beamed.

"Better!"

"Break it up, you four!" Helene said, coming in for a hug. She whispered in Claire's ear. "You've made me the happiest mama in the world. My baby's coming home, and I'm getting another wonderful daughter-in-law. His dad would be so pleased."

"Aw, that means a lot. I love you too, Helene."

Natalie and Jack arrived next. As her mom hugged Ryan for the thousandth time, Claire's future stepfather gave her a side hug.

"I think your mom is more excited about your wedding than ours." He winked. "Congrats, Claire."

"Thanks, Jack. But don't worry. Tomorrow is all about you two, and it's going to be perfect."

He squeezed her shoulder. "It already is."

Mr. Dunlap, standing at the head of the room, cleared his throat. "I believe we're ready to get started."

As everyone took their seats, Ryan grasped Claire's hand. "Are you ready, sweetheart?"

"Let's do this."

After their early morning meeting with the lawyer, Claire felt confident in their plan. The park was a risk, but with them both on board full-time, she believed they would succeed.

"Our plan appears simple," she said after the preliminaries. "Compromise. But that one word is harder than it seems. Pony Island has

Chapter Thirty-Five: Claire

been my dream as much as it was my grandmother's, and the idea of changing even one thing felt like a betrayal. That is, until Ryan showed me the possibilities."

"On the surface," Ryan took over, "Pony Island is an amusement park, a place of summer fun. After graduation, I was in such a hurry to see the world that I forgot how special it was. Coming back, and spending time with Claire, reminded me of the magic this place has over both young and old. It's a part of this community and a fixture of the island." He paused to look each person in the eye. "It would be a shame to see it close."

"Our plan," Claire said, "is to make upgrades to the park as the budget permits, and we're asking for your help. We believe these changes will attract more visitors while keeping the original flavor of the park." She held up a clicker. "We stayed up late to prepare this show for you."

As they led the group through their ideas, including estimates and feasibility studies, Claire spotted smiles, nods, and a few tears. At the end, Mr. Dunlap returned to the front.

"I believe I speak for all of us when I say how impressed I am with these two." The applause began with him and radiated out until the whole room shook with a standing ovation. A familiar woman walked forward.

"I'll take it from here, Lawrence."

The lawyer ceded the floor to Miss Hattie who grinned like the Cheshire cat. Claire and Ryan exchanged a glance, and he playfully nodded toward the exit.

Oh no, you don't! she telepathed, narrowing her eyes.

"On behalf of the Pony Island Corporation, party of one," she said, holding up one finger as those in the know chuckled, "I release to you the interest account set up in 1970 by your grandparents and put in my capable hands." She winked. "But don't get too excited. It started with a dollar."

When Claire saw the amount, her throat constricted. It wouldn't save the park completely, but it was a plenty good start. No wonder the PIC promised to match funds.

"Thank you, Miss Hattie," she said, hugging her friend. "We had no idea it was you!"

"As it should be."

"Is that why you were spying on us last night?" Ryan asked, wrapping her in a bear hug.

"That's for me to know and you to wonder, isn't it?"

"Miss Hattie!"

"There goes my retirement cruise!" the sly woman shouted, heading into the crowd.

"Oh, come on, Miss Hattie! You'll never retire!" Ryan yelled, to the amusement of the room.

"Not now!" she volleyed back. "I don't want to miss this new chapter."

As the meeting wound down, Jacob and Morgan came to the front, her with a hug for Claire and him with a handshake for Ryan.

"We should totally double date!" Morgan said, clapping her hands. Jacob's jaw dropped. "Oh, c'mon, Jake. It would be fun!"

"Yeah, *Jake*," Claire said, emphasizing his nickname. The boy gave her a shy smile.

"What the girlfriend wants…" he began.

"The girlfriend gets," Ryan finished, crossing his arms. "Man, you've got it bad."

"Looks like you do too, sir." When Ryan shook off the formality, Jacob continued eagerly. "Congrats, man, Miss Claire!"

"You too." She turned to Morgan. "I know it's a lot to think about, but we would be honored if you would continue on with us after school starts. We'll work out a fair wage…for both of you."

"Yes!" the girl cried, throwing her arms around both Claire and Ryan.

"Yeah, Miss Claire!" Jacob said, reaching for Morgan's hand. "This

Chapter Thirty-Five: Claire

place is special."

Claire squealed at her happy blush. "Aw, you two are the cutest!"

After they walked away, Ryan leaned over. "No, honey, that would be us. I won't be upstaged by a pair of teenagers."

"Oh, you. Come here," she said, throwing her arms around his neck. *And if the man didn't swoop me down in Times Square victory, well, I'll never tell!*

Squawk! (Let's get this party started!)

"Reynaldo? What are you doing in here?!"

If the little booger didn't wink...

"Claire," Ryan whispered, "let someone else handle the bird. You're busy."

Squawk! (Out of my way, peasants!)

"Claire!" Kendra cried. "We need your...oh! Never mind!"

"Yeah," Claire breathed, brushing her lips over Ryan's, "I *am* pretty busy."

Chapter Thirty-Six: Ryan

11:00 pm

Ryan: You're going to kill me, but...
Dominic: Haven't found a caterer?
Ryan: Worse.
Dominic: I like where this is going.
Ryan: Only you would say that.
Dominic: Gonna tell me? Or do I have to drag it out of you?
Ryan: *selfie of epic post-engagement kiss*
Dominic: TMI, man. I did NOT need to see that.
Ryan: LOL
Dominic: Congratulations! When's the big day?
Ryan: Soon, I hope.
Dominic: I can see that. Taylor says congrats too.
Ryan: Tell her thanks. Now, about Michael's March. What about food trucks?
Dominic: How do you mean?
Ryan: Claire and I had an *amazing* food truck lunch in Savannah. We're adding some of our finds to the park menu, and it got me thinking, why not invite food trucks to Michael's March? We could issue each

Chapter Thirty-Six: Ryan

guest a certain number of vouchers to be redeemed for small plates.

Dominic: Can we afford that?

Ryan: I've run the numbers, and yes, we can. The trucks would also accept cash or charge for additional orders.

...

...

...

Dominic: I discussed it with the others, and we all love the idea! Good job, man! Now, how do we find the trucks?

...

Dominic: Earth to Ryan.

Ryan: Sorry. Claire called to say goodnight. I got a few names from the chefs we met. Three are interested in the gig.

Dominic: Awesome! Don't know what we'll do without you next year. Tell Claire she's one lucky girl.

Ryan: I'm the lucky one. She's...everything.

Dominic: *eyeroll* Keep it to yourself, dude.

* * *

The morning of Jack and Natalie's engagement party-wedding was a flurry of activity. Decorations, flowers, catering, the cake...it all made Ryan's head spin. *If all this is for a second marriage, what will a first one be like?*

Catching sight of Claire in his new favorite of her dresses, a bold vermilion that showed his fiancée's hourglass figure to full advantage... he let out a low whistle when he reached her red espadrilles. *Why haven't we set a date? Late summer, early fall...that could work.*

"Hey, Bro, a little help here?"

"Sorry," Ryan said, helping Travis with the tables. "How long was your engagement, again?"

"Too long," his brother replied, smiling over at Kendra, "but it was worth it. She's going to be an amazing…" He cut off. "Anyway, I think this is the last table."

The ceremony and reception were to be held in the park's outdoor event pavilion, one side of which faced the Atlantic Ocean. A salty zephyr blew through, cooling Ryan's skin as Claire hurried up.

"You two," she said, pointing at the Lanier brothers, "I need you on chair duty. Eight at each table. Then, there are tablecloths, centerpieces, and oh my, do we need chair covers? Let me go ask Mom."

Sixteen chairs later, Claire tugged on Ryan's arm. "Come on, Muscles. I need a strong man to help me with the tubs. Trav, not that you're not strong, but I need you to keep doing chairs."

Travis saluted. Ryan followed her over to the storage building. She located the chair covers, three tubs full, and pulled him behind a shelf.

"This shirt is killing me," she hissed, tracing the 'S' with her finger. "You're taking it on our honeymoon."

"Speak for yourself, doll." She relaxed into his arms, her soft curves tempting him to explore. *Soon. Soon. Soon.* "You're a knockout in this dress. It's coming too. But I've been meaning to ask, what's with all the red?"

"During World War II, red was the color of *victory*."

"Oh," he said, grinning like a shark in Claire-infested waters, "I get it now."

"I don't want a long engagement, hot stuff. How do you feel about late August?"

"You read my mind." He pecked her scarlet lips, wiping his mouth with a growl. "Why are you wearing lipstick?"

She pushed out of his arms and pointed to a tub. "Because, Mr. Lanier, we have work to do. Chop, chop."

He tweaked her side before hefting one. "Spoilsport. But I'll catch you later, Mrs. Soon-to-Be-Lanier."

Chapter Thirty-Six: Ryan

"Not if I catch you first!"

* * *

The party started at 3:00, and by 3:15, the preacher announced the new Mr. and Mrs. Jack Allison. Ryan listened to the ceremony, but he kept straying toward the beauty standing next to the bride...not that Mrs. Hensley-now-Allison wasn't lovely in her own right. But it was more than Claire's lavender dress, chosen to coordinate with the purple foxgloves she'd needlessly panicked over. Ryan was there when that went down.

"I thought we were getting purple delphiniums," Natalie said as the flowers arrived. "These are foxgloves."

"I know, Mom," Claire replied, wringing her hands. Ryan wanted to reach out to her, but he felt this was better left between the mother and daughter. "The florist wasn't able to get the delphiniums, so I substituted the foxgloves. I forgot why they were special to you until it was too late. Are you mad?"

"Oh, sweetheart, no!" Her mom fingered a purple bloom. "It's true they were special for your father and me, but sharing them with Jack doesn't make me mad. You know, it's as if your father is sending his blessing."

Claire wrapped her arm around her mother's shoulders. "I'm sure he would. He thought the world of Jack, and Jack's family is pleased too."

In the present, Ryan watched Claire's expressions like he would a cascade of shooting stars – *I don't want to miss a moment*. When she smiled, the world came alive. When she teared up, he knew she was happy her mother was no longer alone. When she turned all dreamy, he wanted to believe it was because of him.

As the rings were exchanged, she snuck a peek and caught him staring. He winked, relishing the blush spreading up her soft neck.

Her eyelashes kissed her cheek, but it was her spark that sent his heart racing. What at first was an impossible situation was now the biggest blessing of his life.

After much discussion with Claire, Ryan contacted his bosses in Nashville. Due to the nature of his job, telecommuting wasn't possible, he knew, but he didn't want to up and quit. Plus, until the park was in better financial shape, he and Claire could use the extra income. Taylor, brought into the conference call by her father, provided the solution.

"We have connections with a real estate company in Savannah, Georgia, and I heard recently that they're hiring. With our recommendation, Ryan would be a shoo-in."

He wouldn't hear back until sometime the following week, but his friend told him not to worry. "Ryan, we'll miss you, especially Dom, but we're ecstatic for you and Claire. She seems like a sweet person."

"She is," he replied. "And we're coming to get my stuff, so we'll drop by for a visit. You can show her all your social media tips and tricks."

"You can count on it! And I want to know where she gets all those amazing outfits. My wardrobe is in need of a refresh – a *vintage* refresh!"

Claire agreed, and it was clear to Ryan that the girls would soon become good friends. *It would be hard not to be friends with Claire, though,* he mused. *She's loyal, so smart, and brave. She doesn't back down from a challenge, and she brings out the best in me.*

I sound like a man in love, he told himself, rising to applaud the happy couple. *And I would be 100% right.*

When Claire reached his side, he brought her in for a hug. She rested her head on his chest, watching her mom and new stepdad.

"I can't wait to grow old with you, Ryan."

"Claire, honey," he said, raising her chin, "you'll never be older than me."

Chapter Thirty-Six: Ryan

He pecked her on the nose before going to give his congratulations. The meal of fresh-caught seafood was soon served, followed by the 'I Love You a Chocolatté' cake, which was a big hit. Ryan was as tight as a tick by the end, elbowing Claire when she poked him in the belly.

Once most of the guests had gone home, Travis and Kendra called the families together, their hands clasped, their expressions uncertain. Claire looked to Ryan, but he was also in the dark.

"Kendra and I," Travis said, "have an announcement. We are..."

Even the ocean hushed in anticipation. Everyone leaned forward, not to miss a thing.

"Adopting!"

It took a moment for the word to process, but as soon as it did, Helene pulled her son and daughter-in-law into a tight hug.

"We knew there was something going on with y'all. I can't believe this! I'm going to be a grandmother!"

"You're not upset they won't be biological?" Kendra asked, her forehead wrinkled.

"No, honey," Helene said as agreement spread around the group. "They'll be as much a part of this family as any of us."

"We're going to spoil them rotten!" Claire said, hugging her best friend and future sister-in-law. Ryan clapped his brother on the back, giving him a big hug.

"This is awesome, man! How can we help?"

"You already have," Travis said, bringing to mind the work they had done the other day. Claire pointed out the cleaning. "We had our inspection."

"Which we passed," Kendra added. "Now, we're in the waiting-for-a-call phase, but don't get too eager. It might be several months," she took a rattling inhale, "or years."

"It'll be worth it," Natalie said, squeezing her hands.

"And we'll be here for whatever you need in the meantime," Claire said.

"Thanks, guys," Travis replied, pulling Kendra to his side. "That means more than you know."

* * *

The sun was in bed by the time the space was cleaned up. Claire sent Natalie and Jack home at sunset to start their honeymoon, and the others trickled out with big yawns. Ryan returned from his last trip to the supply building, his surprise in tow, to find Claire staring out at the ocean, heels kicked off and feet propped up on the railing. They were the only ones left from the wedding party, but the park would stay open for another hour.

"Hey there, handsome," she said, doing a double take. "Where'd you get that hat?"

He tipped his black fedora. "You like?"

"You know I do." She fanned herself with one hand. "Pull up a chair, good lookin'."

He held out his hand. "I've got a better idea."

"Shall I reapply my lipstick?"

"Don't you dare!"

He led her hand in hand to the Sand Dollar and exchanged a nod with the operator. As soon as they settled into the seat, Ryan put his arm around Claire.

"What are you up to?" she asked, snuggling in. After a jingle, the ride began its ascent. The glow of the multicolored bulbs reflected off her radiant skin. He forced his attention out to the dark ocean, the full moon smiling on the waters, the stars winking encouragement.

"Making dreams come true."

As soon as they reached the top, the wheel stopped, causing the swing to rock lightly. Starting at her bare shoulder, he traced his finger down

Chapter Thirty-Six: Ryan

her arm. Goosebumps spread like ripples in the water, and he willed his pulse to slow.

She's mine now. No need to rush.

"How long do we have?" she asked, shifting toward him.

"Fifteen minutes."

"Then why," she whispered, wrapping her arm around his neck, "aren't you kissing…"

Eighteen minutes later, they emerged from the ride hand in hand and a little dazed.

"I didn't realize he was going to take us on the full ride afterward," Ryan said.

"That makes eleven more to go."

"Wait! We already kissed in the Widow's Walk. That makes ten, or depressingly, less."

Claire swung their clasped hands. "No, we kissed *behind the scenes* in the Widow's Walk. I'm not counting that."

"What about the drop tower? I love you, darlin', but…plus, I'm not even sure how that would work."

"You forget, there are three 'lighthouses' on Pony Island."

"Ah, I see."

"As for the rides that are closed…and the Loggerheads…we'll improvise."

"As long as I'm with you, Kryptonite."

"Kryptonite?"

He pulled up her contact information. "It's official, honey, and totally accurate. You, Claire Hensley, are my weakness."

She stopped him in the glow of the Rolling Waves. "And you're my strength. Together, we can do…"

"Anything."

Epilogue: Claire

Summer 2049 – Pony Island Amusement Park's Sea-tennial Celebration

"100 years, Mrs. Lanier, and better than ever," Claire's as-*hunky-and-delicious*-as-ever husband said, taking her hand. "Miss Hattie would be so proud."

As usual, she and Ryan were the last ones in the park, soaking up the peace of twilight. Today's centennial celebration went off without a hitch…if one didn't count Reymond's snake-hunting expedition into the garden at Piper's, startling a pair of honeymooners from Oregon.

Reynaldo would be so proud.

"I'm meeting with Morgan in the morning to go over our new ad campaign. How that woman keeps the ideas flowing, especially with those three boys," Claire said as they strolled under the lamplight, "I'll never know."

"I'm sure Jacob's got something to do with it." Ryan nudged her arm. "I know you've kept me young, hot stuff."

"As have you, *Clark*."

The Carou-Sail's lights twinkled a welcome, the restored calliope playing 'The Anniversary Waltz.' As they did on their wedding anniversary each year, tonight on the park's, they climbed aboard for a song. Claire sat sidesaddle on her favorite steed, her husband looping his arms around her waist.

"Think Mom, Natalie, and Jack will survive without us?" he asked. "I know Travis and Kendra don't want to miss Kati's first trip overseas."

"Yes, I do. Alice and Kati are thrilled about our European tour," Claire said, thinking of their daughter and niece. "We must squeeze in their favorite sites in between the business stops." She laughed softly. "Who knew visiting other amusement parks would be so much work?"

"I have a few sights I want to squeeze in," Ryan replied, his greying beard tickling her neck.

"Ryan!"

"Hey, now! It's not what you think...exactly." He nipped at her ear. "Since we haven't been on a trip by ourselves in far too long, I've made a few arrangements. A little side excursion, of sorts, while the others go...elsewhere." His deep laugh rumbled to her toes as he caressed her thigh. "On second thought, sugar, it's exactly what you think."

"I think it sounds perfect."

As they shared a kiss honed with time, the song reached its peak. Ryan pulled Claire from her perch to sing the final lines of 'The Anniversary Waltz' together.

"You're my real romance, Ryan Lanier, my dream come true, through all the smiles and tears. There's no one I'd rather dance through life with than you."

Squawk! (Your hero has arrived!)

"Get along home, Reymond!" Ryan yelled, dipping his head. "This girl's mine-all-mine."

About the Author

Lizzy James is a pen name of Elizabeth J. Smith, an author of fiction with a Christian worldview. She spent one semester in college working in food service at a big-name amusement park and used some of her own experiences as *inspiration* (*not actual events*) for *Do I Look Amused?* (Shoutouts to the leaky pink slushie machine! Never thought I'd be grateful for those two long hours.) She and Claire have a lot in common, including a love of 1940s fashion and lifestyle, lighthouses, and the delightful feel of a coastal breeze. And like Ryan, she loves food trucks and will happily skip the drop tower! When she's not writing or editing, she loves being outside, reading, and baking.

Elizabeth is married to her college sweetheart (also an amusement park alum), and they have one beautiful (adopted) daughter. She is also the author of the **Harriford Grange** series, Christian historical romance short stories, and the **Maripi Moon** series, young adult science fiction. She uses the pen name Lizzy James for her light and fun romantic comedies.

You can connect with me on:

- https://authorelizabethjsmith.com
- https://twitter.com/authorejsmith
- https://www.facebook.com/authorelizabethjsmith
- https://www.instagram.com/authorelizabethjsmith

Also by Lizzy James

For Your Amusement Sweet Romantic Comedies
Do I Look Amused?
You Amuse Me - Coming 2023

Made in the USA
Monee, IL
29 August 2022